Eye of t.

Charlotte Koyle
5th class
St. Mary N.S.
0879129811

Eye of the Cannon

Sam Llewellyn

CATNIP BOOKS
Published by Catnip Publishing Ltd.
Islington Business Centre
3-5 Islington High Street
London N1 9LQ

This edition published 2007
1 3 5 7 9 10 8 6 4 2

A CIP catalogue record for this book is available from the British
Library

ISBN 978-1-84647-020-2

Printed in Poland

www.catnippublishing.co.uk

Contents

Surgeon's Knot

On the most unusual day of her life, Kate Griffiths got up in the morning as usual. As usual, she splashed her face with cold water from the basin on the stand and raked a horn comb through her just-short-of-the-shoulder tangle of red hair. She made a face at herself in the mirror. Her Aunt Megan said her hair was too frizzy, her nose too short, her mouth too wide, and her eyes green as poison. Kate did not give a monkey's bum for what her Aunt Megan thought. Her Aunt Megan and Uncle Owen had looked after her since her parents had emigrated to America. There had been one letter from them since they had gone what seemed to Kate an age ago. Megan said that both of them had by now undoubtedly been eaten by Indians. Kate took this as a further example of the rubbish Megan talked.

Kate was unusually tired that morning. But

she knew she had to get out of the house before Megan woke up and gave her some disgusting job to do. So she rolled out of bed and climbed into her ankle-length dress of grey flannel and did up the tapes on her pinafore, pulling the bows extra tight to show how much she loathed Megan.

A grey light was struggling over the black slates of Pembroke and through the diamond panes of the attic window. The sound of snoring filtered through the floor. Outside, horses' hooves clattered. Kate peered out. The milk cart was crawling down the cobbled street, small as a model. She looked away; she did not like heights. As usual, she took her shoes in her hand so the sound of her leather soles would not kick up a clatter on the stairs. The snoring grew louder, long and piggish, rattling the planks of the black door on the landing, behind which Megan lay sleeping with her mouth open. Kate scuttled down the staircase. The shop was on the ground floor. In the back scullery, her uncle, Owen Griffiths the barber–surgeon, was bent in a cloud of steam over the zinc basin in which he was washing his saws and scalpels and tweezers, ready for the day's work. She ducked down, keeping the brown leather barber's chair between her and her uncle, and ran into the street.

It had rained in the night. On the doorstep,

under the red-and-white pole in front of the shop, she paused to put on her shoes against the muck on the cobbles.

A medium-sized voice by her left foot said, "Braow?"

A cat was sitting on the bottom step, staring at her with large, irritable green eyes. It was tied to the boot scraper with a length of tarred twine.

Kate liked cats. She sat down on the damp doorstep and said, "What are you doing here?"

The cat gave her a look expressive of deep scorn. It was, the look said, perfectly obvious what it was doing. Someone had tied it to a boot scraper with a series of elaborate knots, which probably looked quite impressive to a human child, but which were in the cat's view undignified, not to say positively humiliating. Would Kate please untie them immediately, if not sooner?

Kate patted it. The cat turned its attention to a bit of shredded paper near its right paw. It batted the paper into a puddle. Round its neck, attached to the string collar, was another, smaller scrap of paper. There was writing on it.

Kate nearly did not give it a second thought. But her eyes were strangely anchored to it, drawn by the same mysterious process that makes your name jump out at you from a page.

For the scrap of paper said:

MISTRESS KATE GR—

She examined it more closely. The paper on the collar looked like a label, most of which had been torn off. Kate realized that the piece of paper in the puddle was the rest of the label. She fished it out. There had been three or four lines of writing on it; but the ink had run, and was now flowing down the gutter towards Milford Haven.

The cat said, "Braow?" again. There was definitely an accusing note in its voice.

Kate looked up and down the street. It was empty. From the pocket of her pinafore she pulled the large horn-handled sailor's clasp knife that was one of her dearest possessions. She cut the string, and sat the cat in her lap. She did it with some difficulty, because it was the biggest cat she had ever seen, and seemed to weigh as much as one of Aunt Megan's water buckets, the ones she had to fill at the well before breakfast each day. It had immensely long fur, and paws the size of Uncle Owen's biggest shaving brushes.

As well as being the biggest cat she had ever seen, she decided, it was the most beautiful. The blood quickened in her veins. And it had arrived on the doorstep, with most of a label addressed to her tied round its neck.

Nobody gave Kate anything, ever, except the clout-round-the-ear-for-being-slow-with-the-slop-bucket kind of thing. Kate possessed her books, her clasp knife, a few clothes, the last letter her parents had sent, and (if you believed Megan) an expensive habit of eating food. And that was that.

Kate hugged the cat.

The cat put its paws on her shoulders and hugged her back.

Wheels rang on the cobbles. She folded her knife and slid it quickly into her pocket.

Gwyn the ropemaker was passing at the helm of a cartload of stinking hemp fibres. "Good morning, Mistress Kate," he said with the blubbery smirk he reserved for meek little red-haired orphans who knew their place. He ignored the cat. Cats were beneath his notice.

"Good morning, sir," she said, and curtseyed, because Gwyn was one of Megan's sneaks and spies, and a curtsey now could save a clout on the ear later.

Gwyn rode away, cart wheels rattling. Kate gazed after him with the sweet smile she used instead of sticking her tongue out. Then she put on her normal face, tucked the cat under her arm, and went to get two hot buns and a joke from jolly

Mrs Jones the bakery, who hated Megan. The cat drank a saucer of milk while Mrs Jones the bakery made polite remarks about its beauty, and rude ones about Megan.

Mrs Jones was a comfort to Kate in a very uncomfortable world. She looked much as a baker should, with a white apron, a red face well dusted with flour, and wooden pattens that clattered like musket-shots on the brick floor of the bakery. But her bakerishness was not the thing that made Kate like her.

The thing Kate principally liked about Mrs Jones was that she had known her father, and was not afraid to talk about him. All Kate remembered of him was a lot of red hair, a pair of hands that made mighty gestures and a confused roaring noise that might or might not have been speech. Her mother she remembered better. There had been a dreadful time three years before, when Mama had wept for a week, given a purse of money to Megan and another to Ann Murley the schoolmistress, and left for America, saying that she was to join Kate's father, and that she would send word soon.

There had been the one letter. After that no word had ever come, despite Kate's anguished hoping.

So this morning, she had something in particular to ask Mrs Jones' advice about.

It had been last night. She had eaten the remains of Owen and Megan's supper, as usual. She had washed the dishes, scoured the pots, filled the water churn from the well, scrubbed the kitchen floor, snuffed the candles, and taken her tallow dip to her garret. And there she had read the books that had come with the last letter, after her mother had gone down to the Dock and stepped aboard the packet boat.

They were large and splendid books, with pictures of copper-coloured Indians with feathers in their hair, wearing long coats with gold braid at wrist and hem. There were forests, mountains and gorges, and an engraving of a town that looked half-finished, called Baltimore. Kate had no idea why her parents had sent those particular books. There was no explanation in the letter, which said they were well, and hoped she was likewise, and told her to be patient. It did not occur to her to ask anyone. Her mother had spoken of her father as a wild person, a poet, given to doing wonderful things for no reason. When she had spoken of him, there had been an odd look in her eye: half lit-up, Kate thought, and half nervous. Megan's view was simpler. She disapproved of him thoroughly. She also disapproved of Kate's mother, her sister-in-law, for being alive; and she disapproved of Kate because Kate was allowed to go to school, when she should have been spending all her time cleaning the house.

This state of general disapproval had lasted two years. But since last night, it looked as if a change was in store.

The voices had come up through the floorboards late, when Kate should have been asleep. Megan had been abnormally vicious all evening. Kate had heard her name mentioned. She had crept out of bed, stuck her ear to the rough planks.

"So that's settled," Megan was saying. It was one of her favourite phrases.

Uncle Owen made mewing sounds. Megan was not an easy person to argue with.

"Peace, husband!" said Megan. "Cardiff's a splendid town, look. Flowing with money. Trade, industry, look. Injured people galore. And no expenses, because the girl Kate will do for a servant. It's about time."

More mewing.

"I've sweated blood over that girl," said Megan sharply. "School every day, look, like Lady La-di-da. Well, that's over. She'll learn to work for her living. And we'll break her spirit. Oh, yes, we will. A month from now, off we go. That's settled."

More mewing.

"Quiet," said Megan, sharp as a whip.

Three minutes later, she was snoring.

Kate lay awake until the dawn was grey in the diamond-paned windows.

She knew what would happen in Cardiff. School kept her free. Without school, away from people she knew, Megan could do what she liked. And Kate would land in some back kitchen, half underground, scouring cooking pots with bunches of chain and caustic soda, watching the green mould grow on the walls. You might as well be buried alive.

So she said to Mrs Jones the bakery, "I think Uncle and Aunt are moving away."

Mrs Jones smiled absent-mindedly, heaving a tray of loaves out of an apprentice's hands and onto a rack. "Shouldn't be surprised," she said.

"To Cardiff."

"That's where the money is, they say."

"I was wondering," said Kate. "Could I ... stay with you?"

Mrs Jones the bakery turned upon her her two little black eyes like currants in a giant, sweaty bun. "Gracious no," she said. "Not that I wouldn't love it, mind. But Megan's your guardian, rot her. Until sent for. So it can't be done."

Kate nodded. She wanted to cry. Someone in the

back was yelling about four dozen mutton pies. "You get along, now," said Mrs Jones the bakery. "You'll survive."

Kate knew there was no use hanging around.

So she tucked the cat under her arm, and got along.

At the bottom of the hill the masts and rigging of a dozen ships made a grid of the dirty-grey morning sky.

Pembroke Dock was full of ships. It was the first stop for merchantmen sailing in from Ireland and America, and a handy repair yard for men-of-war fresh from battering and being battered with cannon in the cold Atlantic. Megan held that real girls were not interested in ships. In the moments when they were not at school or scrubbing pots in the scullery, they were meant to play with dolls, and say la! and fie! at the smell of tar. But Kate loved that smell of tar, and everything else to do with the huge, black-and-buff-painted sailing machines that wallowed in and out of the harbour with the tides. And Kate was a determined person.

Life is not at all easy when to the best of your knowledge your parents live four thousand miles away by sailing ship and footpath, and your uncle–guardian makes his living by performing operations on awake people in the brown leather chair in the shop, and your aunt–guardian keeps you in the house only because you are cheaper than a servant. Some children would undoubtedly have given up, and done precisely what they were told.

Not Kate.

She knew that her mother had left her behind because of the dangers of the new country. The letter said so. *It is hard, being separate from us, and we from you,* said the letter. *But we will one day be united. Till then, patience.* If she had shown it to Megan, Megan would have said it was nonsense, and given her the pewter candlesticks to burnish with sand, to get such pish and flummery out of her mind. She knew that whatever Megan said, the pair of them were still alive, and getting things ready for her first visit to their new home in America. And she knew that one day, she was not clear how, they would send for her, and that would be that.

Kate was confident as well as determined. And the further away from Megan she went, the more confident she got.

Still clasping the cat, she wove her way through the crowds, up the hill, holding up her pinafore, remembering to skip instead of run as she wanted to. The cat looked here and there, showing a lively interest in the proceedings. At the bottom she turned under a crumbling stone arch, through a yard full of timber waiting to be transformed into ships' planking, and into a blacksmith's shop. It was behind the blacksmith's shop that Kate stepped into the secret part of her life.

2

Slippery Hitch

It was half-dark in the shop. Dewi the smith was still in bed, still drunk from last night's gin hot with. Charley the boy was there, picking sleep out of his eyes and coughing on the embers of the forge. Doctor Morgan did not like Charley's cough; but nobody was paying for Charley's food, let alone doctors to look after Charley. So Doctor Morgan not liking the cough was as far as it went.

As usual, Kate gave Charley one of her buns, and ate the other. Then, also as usual, she scuttled round the back of the forge. She carried the cat – not without effort, because it really was heavy – up a ladder into a loft full of old blankets. From a cupboard she took a bundle of clothes. Pulling off her pinafore and dress, she stepped into a pair of canvas breeches, a red flannel shirt and seaboots. The cat took a nap on the blankets. She wondered whether she should leave it there for safety while she decided what to do with it. Aunt Megan would chase it away or drown it. She twisted her hair into a pigtail, smeared forge soot on her face and hands. The cat said, "Braow?"

Megan had made sure that Kate did not have many friends. The cat seemed to be a friend. She decided that she simply could not leave it. She hoisted it under her arm and slid down the ladder. Then, transformed, as every day off, into a boy of about twelve, she headed for the harbour.

Gwyn the rope maker had dumped his load of hemp at the ropewalk. He was smoking a short clay pipe, leaning on a barrel by the dockyard gates. Kate made herself walk straight past him without hesitating. He paid no attention to a red-haired cabin boy with a dirty face and a huge cat. Cabin boys were two a penny in Pembroke Dock, and cats were the next best thing to invisible to citizens as important as Gwyn. Even at this hour of the morning the yard was a boiling soup of people and animals, but Kate did not let them distract her. She knew exactly where she was going.

Kate was extremely interested in ships. Perhaps in the back of her mind was the idea that they brought her in some way closer to her father. In the front of her mind, she loved the magic by which trees turned into boats, and boats went on the water.

They were building a big ketch on the West Slip. By the side of the dock, the sparmakers were finishing the mainmast. They had squared off the trunk of a Douglas fir brought from the far forests of Upper Canada. Then they had planed the corners off the beam, to make it eight-sided. After that they had smoothed off the facets with planes and spokeshaves until what remained was a tapering cylinder of honey-gold wood.

Kate had watched the whole process. It had taken three weeks. She spent most of her spare moments down here in the dockyards, watching. At first she had worn her own clothes. But Gwyn had reported to the Reverend Pugh that she had been seen hanging around with rough workmen. The Reverend Pugh had had a quiet word in Megan's ear after Chapel, and Megan had whipped her with the strop Barber Griffiths used to sharpen his razors. Barber Griffiths had looked the other way, red and uncomfortable.

So Kate had cut off most of her hair. Megan had been furious again, but Kate had pointed out that long hair only got greasy in the kitchen. Then she had pulled one shilling and sixpence, her life savings, from under her bed and bought herself a set of boy's clothes from Moss's Emporium by the dock gate. Filthy dirty, and with her hair in a pigtail, she passed for a cabin boy off one of the ships in the Haven, and no one took a blind bit of notice of her.

This morning, the mastmakers were due to fit the iron hoop to which would be attached the rigging that would keep the mast upright. Kate settled the cat across her shoulders, and gave them her full attention.

The sparmakers had a portable forge, with a brazier of red-hot charcoal. The hoop was resting on the coals, glowing the colour of a cherry in the grey morning light. The gaffer took a pair of tongs from a rack, picked up the hoop, gave it a couple of whangs on the anvil, quenched it in a trough of water, and walked towards the mast.

Hooves rattled behind her. "Hey!" said a voice behind Kate. "You!"

The cat jumped down into her arms. She froze. If someone recognized her, it would be a whipping. Worse, it would be the end of the cat, and the end of freedom. Megan would make the most of an excuse not to let her out of the house again. She would make her a house slave in the dark scullery with its stone sink and damp green walls. She did not turn round. Carefully, the gaffer applied the warm iron to the mast. She watched intently, caught up in the suspense—

"Hey!" said the voice again. This time, there was a crack and a stinging pain in her right ear. Tears came to her eyes. She spun round.

There was a carriage and pair. On the box was a man with a coachman's many-caped overcoat and coal-black teeth, swishing the whip with which he had flicked her ear. Behind the glass of the window, a man's face looked out, dull and fat-lipped. Beside it was the face of a boy. The eyes were blue and furious, like a pig's. "Werry accurate, me," said the coachman, laying his finger alongside his brandy-purple nose. " 'Old the 'osses, eh, boy?"

Kate had never seen him before. She felt a surge of relief, and opened her mouth to tell him to hold them himself. But longshoreboys did not say things like that where there might be a ha'penny in it. Nor did eleven-year-old girls like Kate Griffiths.

So she put up the hand that was not holding the cat, and took the reins.

"I'm looking for a ship," said the coachman. "The *Narwhal*."

Kate knew how to deal with officious grown-ups; she had had practice. She let her jaw drop, and unfocused her eyes so they looked like bleary grey-green stones. The *Narwhal* was an eight-gun sloop of war, captured from the French two months ago, which had just finished a refit. She had watched most of the work. But she was not about to do anything to help people who flicked her ear with whiplashes in this crowd, where someone might recognize her voice.

The coachman frowned. He peered into her face, saw no gleam of intelligence, grunted and strode off. Kate wanted to concentrate on the sparmakers. The reins were in the way. She wrapped the reins a couple of times round an iron railing, tied a sort of one-handed knot, and forced her way to the front of the crowd. She was an independent person, studying the sea trade, her trusty cat across her shoulders. She had watched ships being built from keel to maintruck. One of these days – she was not entirely clear how – she would go to sea, and continue her education. In time, this skill would enable her to cross the Atlantic, to look for her parents.

Not just yet, of course; for it was 1813, and for reasons not clear to her, the English were at war with the Americans as well as the French. The Irish Sea was rumoured to be crawling with American privateers – fast ships carrying licences called letters of marque that permitted them to chase, capture and sell the ships of enemy nations. But war did not last for ever. At least, Kate hoped not.

The gaffer sparmaker had detected a misfit. He had pulled off the iron ring, and walloped it again on the anvil. Now, sweating from the heat and weight, he plunged into a bucket of water. There was a roar and a hiss and a cloud of steam. The cat wriggled out of Kate's arms and darted off into the crowd. Her concentration was broken. She gave a yell, and started off after it. Over to her left there was a commotion, and a horse whinnied.

Things began to happen.

Across the sea of heads she could see the coach horses rearing and plunging. Her heart was in her throat, and not only because the cat had gone. In fact, the cat suddenly seemed strangely unimportant.

She began to burrow back through the crowd to the railings. You did not tie up a team of horses. Everyone knew that. She should have been holding them. She hoped the knot was all right.

Suddenly, the horses wheeled. There was a lot of shouting now. Some of it was coming from inside the coach. The coach began to move.

With a nasty, sick feeling, Kate realized that the knot had been far from all right.

3

Locking Turn

As the carriage hurtled down the cobbled quay towards the dock gates, two things happened. First, the doors burst open, and a boy jumped out. He was running before his feet touched the ground. It was the boy whose eyes Kate had seen at the window. She caught a glimpse of a mean, white face and carrot-red hair before he disappeared into the crowd.

Next there was a tremendous bellow. A man heaved himself into the carriage doorway, balancing clumsily against the rock of the vehicle. He was a fat man with huge white breeches and a blue jacket. His was the dull, bloated face that had been goggling from the window. Now it was purple with rage. He was roaring, "Come back!" and shaking his fist after the boy. The boy did not come back. The man jumped.

He was too fat to be jumping out of moving carriages. Before he could take a step, he had tripped over his feet and fallen flat on his face. There was a dreadful *snap* as the rear carriage wheel went over his leg. He began to bellow in real earnest, the kind of bellowing Kate heard all too often floating up from Barber Griffiths' shop as she read the books about America in her room.

People gathered round. "Broke 'is leg," said the gaffer sparmaker.

There were beads of sweat on the fat man's face. The ruddiness had gone from it. Now it was as white as lard. Kate felt giddy with misery. This was all her fault; it was her knot that had given way. She wanted to say, Bring him up to our house, my uncle's the barber–surgeon, he'll help. But the man's face was pale and terrifying, and she was so sick with guilt that she could not speak. Also, she was in her boy's clothes, and if she was found out, her life was over.

A gruff voice said, "Someone fetch Surgeon Griffiths."

She slid away before she could be chosen to run the errand. Her uncle would recognize her, even if no one else did. Besides, she had to find the cat.

Then she heard a horse whinny. The carriage had not stopped moving after it had run over the man. Now, on the flat, cobbled top of the quay, the horses were running wild.

As Kate fought her way past the coat-skirts of the crowd towards somewhere with a better view, there was a deep gasp, followed by a big, complicated crash. A bollard loomed up in the forest of legs. She jumped on its top. Once she was up there she wished she had stayed on the ground.

The carriage had swiped the window of Morgan's chandler's and knocked down the pile of barrels outside the Green Dragon brewery. The brown edge of a river of beer was flowing past Kate's feet, heading for the quay.

The shouting roared round Kate's head like a hurricane. *All because she had dressed up as a boy, and tied a slippery hitch.*

She stood on her bollard, striving to be invisible, like a bittern in the reeds.

Between the heads of the crowd, she caught the coachman's eye.

Something had knocked his hat down onto his nose. His face was blue-black with fury. "Orrhh!" he yelled, like an animal. "Wait'll I ketch you! Orrhh!" And he began to lumber towards her.

She slid into the crowd. Behind her, a new kind of shouting started.

She began running. Her heart was hammering.

She was so terrified that her head had gone completely empty. Oh, no, she thought. Oh, dear. Where can I go?

In a cliff of stacked boxes she saw a slot. The mouth of an alley. She dived in.

It was narrow enough for her shoulders to touch the sides. Far too narrow for the coachman, with his stomach and his capes.

The alley ended in a sort of square, two yards by two. In the middle of the square was a bollard.

On the bollard sat the cat. It was licking its paws to wash behind its ears. It gave Kate an impatient green-eyed look as if to say, What kept you? Then it carried on being greyish-brown, striped like a tiger, big and solid. On the ends of its ears were pointed tufts of fur, like the tufts on the ears of a lynx that she had seen in a book of Mr Bewick's engravings. Altogether it was a vast and peculiar cat, and it stuck up like a lighthouse in the panicky gloom of Kate's mind.

The cat slid down from the bollard, looking over its shoulder at Kate as if it wanted her to follow. Then it cantered off into a wafer-thin slot between two piles of timber, tail waving like a flag.

Kate ran after it. The sky was a thin grey ribbon overhead. The cat looked round again, as if to check she was following. It ran down an alley just wide enough for its whiskers, turned through a maze of bales and barrels, and skipped through the skeleton of a half-built boat. Suddenly, it came out on to a quay.

Kate was panting. There was a ship alongside the quay. It was a spruce, tidy-looking ship, floating on the top of the flood tide. Its sides were painted in alternate buff and black rectangles. The rigging that supported its three towering masts was neatly tarred, tensioned and knotted with a perfection for which Kate, even fleeing an angry crowd, could not help feeling a professional admiration.

She knew the ship, just as she knew every ship that berthed in the docks. It was His Majesty King George's three-masted sloop-of-war *Narwhal*, to which the coachman had been asking directions. Just now, she looked deserted.

Something hummed past Kate's ear and shattered on one of the stones of the quay. The cat leaped high into the air, wailed horribly, bounced into the ship and sprinted up the rigging like a streak of furry lightning.

"Blast," said a voice on the ship.

It belonged to a boy in dirty white breeches, sitting on the roof of a deckhouse. He had a sour brown face, and a catapult in his hand. He looked at Kate with his close-together eyes, turned scornfully away and slouched through a door in the deckhouse.

The rigging went up from the ship's rail like a ladder. There was a dull roar of shouting in Kate's ears, like the roar of the surf in the rocks of Angle Bay. The boy was below decks. There would be other people there. She could not afford to meet other people just now. She thought of the cat. Above her head the clouds had split and a breeze was humming in the great empty spiderweb of the rigging. In front of her, the shrouds went up from the quayside like a rope ladder. She stepped across the narrow gap of dirty water and started to climb.

She climbed hard for perhaps ten seconds. Then she glanced between her feet, and her stomach swooped, and her knees turned to jelly.

Everything was very small. The deck looked the size of a leaf. The fat golden mast tapered away to nothing. It was all a long, long way down.

Above her, something said, "Braow?"

She looked up. The cat's furry face was gazing at her over the edge of a platform; the maintop, Kate knew it was called. The sight of it gave her courage, but not enough courage to climb.

Then the shouting came closer. There was one voice above the others. A big voice.

It roared, "I'll 'ave 'is 'ide for a snot rag, swelp me!"

A new terror strengthened Kate's legs. If she went down, she would be caught. Up here, she was just another ship's boy, climbing the rigging. Nobody but a ship's boy would be clambering around up here between earth and sky. The cat watched her, purring and winking its eyes, first one, then the other.

After what seemed like half an hour, she reached the platform. "Puss," she said, through dry lips. "Mog, mog, pussy."

The cat miaowed, and skipped lightly up the next set of shrouds. Kate saw it was limping. Poor thing, she thought, hot with anger against the catapultist. She looked over the edge of the platform and sat back quickly.

Far below, like the crater of a volcano, was the pink bald spot in the centre of the head of the coachman. The coachman was shaking his head, and making baffled gestures with the swollen hands at the ends of the sleeves of his many-caped coat.

She sat with her back against the good solid mast, and her whitish shins stuck out below her breeches. Megan would have exploded with shame. But up here, there was no Megan. There was only a ship's boy, invisible.

The sun was hot. The sounds of the town were a dull roar below. It seemed like days since she had crept from her garret in her grey flannel dress and pinafore.

She sat back to wait.

The cat perched on the next yard above, and watched her. Up on the maintop, Kate watched it back.

The maintop was a big platform, bathed in sun. You could see the rows of houses on the hills above the harbour, the topmasts of the other ships in the dock. There was no sensation of height.

The sounds of the world below were a drowsy hum. It had been a late night, the night before. No, thought Kate. It would be stupid to go to sleep up here.

But her eyelids were as heavy as boulders.

Must get up, thought Kate. Must …

She dozed.

In her doze, there were sounds: creaking and thumping, shouts, the rush of bare feet on wood. The cat laughed at her in a furry voice, Ho ho. Even in her sleep it struck her that this was unusual. So she woke up.

It was not the cat laughing at her. It was a man not much taller than her, but about four times as wide. He looked as if he had been carved out of oak, this man. He was hanging on a rope that plunged diagonally from far aloft. His arm was tattooed with a mermaid, three anchors, and a sheaf of daggers. As he shifted position on the rope, she saw he had a pigtail, stiffened with black tar and crisscrossed with intricate knots, which hung all the way down to the broad leather belt of his bell-bottom trousers.

She was still half asleep, but the fear rose in her like a tide. With a mouth made stiff by nerves, she said, "Pray, who are you?"

He pursed his lips into a parrot's beak. "Who pray am I? I am Jago. You will of heard on me."

"I'm afraid not," said Kate. Something was wrong. There were men in the rigging, like apples in a leafless tree. On the two yards above her, white sails had blossomed against the blue sky.

"Jago's heard on *you*," said the man. His eyes were narrow and glittered like blue steel knives. "Master will-be-capting Fortescue. They sez you are a surly runagates, little Master Fortescue. Your chest come aboard with all yer slops, but we thought as 'ow the owner 'adn't come, which is what, saving yerself, we had been led to believe was a 'abit of yours, Master Fortescue. Until we spotted ye asnoozing in the Rope School. And me, the schoolmaster, *at* your service!" He bowed in mid-air. "So let us proceed in peace, Master Fortescue."

Kate had no idea what he was talking about. Nor did she know why he should think she was called Fortescue. She sat up, to ask the better. Her eye slipped over the edge of the maintop. Her heart seemed to roll in her chest. She sat back again, very quickly.

Last time she had looked down there had been the quay, carts rattling, cranes loading boxes, the clatter of heels on cobblestones.

It had all gone.

Now there was blue water, squeezed to foam by the hull of the ship. To port and starboard, distant blue headlands were falling astern. The ship was leaving the mouth of the Haven as a cannonball leaves the barrel of a gun. Ahead, the horizon was a sharp, dazzling line against the sky.

The *Narwhal* was at sea.

4

Idiot's Delight

Kate said, "There's been a mistake. I'm not Master Fortescue."

Jago smiled at her. His teeth were brilliantly white and his eyes were even bluer than the sea. "That's what a lot of 'em say," he said. "You'll come to love it. Trust old Jago." He swooped onto the platform on his rope. Then to her horror he tucked her under his arm, and launched himself into space. For a moment she could smell him, salt and sweat and old tobacco. Then her stomach was up there in mid-air, and she was screaming, because they were plummeting towards the deck. At the last minute, something happened. They slowed, effortless as a bird braking. Jago landed light as a cat, and set her down with infinite care.

"Welcome aboard the *Narwhal*, Master Fortescue," he said.

There were four boys on the deck. They were wearing whitish breeches and bluish coats. The tallest of them was the boy who had shot at the cat. He might have been twelve. He glanced at Kate with his close-together brown eyes, and became improbably interested in a seagull.

"Mister Bryanston," said Jago. Then he introduced two tiny fair-haired boys. The bigger of them might have been seven. "Masters George and Henry Bean. And Mr Keane."

Keane was the second biggest, about the same age as Kate. He had a brown, boneless-looking face, and black hair that looked as if it had been chewed off short by rats. His eyebrows were thick and black, and they arched over his spaniel-brown eyes like the pause signs in Megan's hymn-book. He looked clever, and there was something about the set of his thin mouth that made Kate think he might be funny. "Now," said Jago. "Which of you gemmen will show Master Fortescue the Palace?"

"Busy," said Bryanston.

Jago smiled sweetly at him, and turned his attention to Keane. "Perhaps you would be so kind," he said. "*Hif* you could spare a moment."

"Golden moments," said Keane. "Nuggets of treasure plucked from the vasty hoard of eternity."

"Talk sense," said Bryanston.

"One day, my pretty Bryanstonia," said Keane, "you may achieve wisdom, and comprehend the utterances of your superiors." He frowned, drawing the large eyebrows together. "But on reflection, I doubt it."

Kate found herself liking Keane.

Bryanston said, "Don't you call me that, squirt. And just you shut your—"

"Gemmen," said Jago, soft as a velvet whip. There was a silence, broken by the sploosh and roar of *Narwhal*'s progress through the ink-blue swells.

"Of course," said Keane. "Let us proceed, Mr Fortescue." He extended his left arm, crooked, the gesture of a gentleman taking a lady in to supper at a ball. Kate nearly took the arm. Then she remembered she was not a girl, and the blood rose to her face.

"Very pretty," said Bryanston, with sarcasm.

"Pay no heed to this scum," said Keane. "Allow me."

He led Kate through a crowd of sailors and through a hatch. There was a flight of steps – a companionway, you called it on a ship – that led down into darkness. It smelt down there: sweat, and the rotten-eggs stink of bilges, and tar from the dockyard. She did not resist. Her head was spinning worse than when she had looked off the maintop down onto the deck. Keep walking, she told herself. You'll think of something. Men passed them on the steps. They arrived in a small cabin, a little wooden room with no windows. A yellow lamp burned in a corner. There were boxes on the floor, casting long black shadows. "The Palace," said Keane, with a courtly flourish of his hand. "Our restaurant. Our hotel. Our Theatre Royal. It's better than it looks. I say, cheer up."

Being told to cheer up made it worse. Kate could feel tears heating up her eyes.

"Bad luck about your pa," said Keane, in a less la-di-da voice. "Breaking his leg, I mean."

She raised her eyes and stared at him. His eyebrows were drawn worriedly together.

"My pa died at sea," he said. "Last voyage but one. The captain kept me on as his personal follower. I suppose they told you what to expect."

"No," said Kate. Her voice was extra small.

"They didn't tell me either," said Keane. "My father just dragged me aboard, and that was that. You spend a bit of time with the schoolmaster, and one day they make you a midshipman, and you get Jack Sprat teaching you to be an officer instead of Jago teaching you how to tie a middy bow. It's not all bad. Captain's a monster and Jack Sprat, he's the first lieutenant, gives the orders, he's a madman. And Bryanston's a pig, of course. But Jago's a pleasant cove, far as I can tell, long as you give satisfaction in the Rope School."

"The Rope School?"

"That's us," said Keane. "Jago arrived a month back, just as we came in Pembroke for fitting-out. He's making us learn things. Captain took him on as schoolmaster. Never had no schoolmaster before he came. We just amused ourselves. Now it's Rope School every morning, rain or shine. Dear dead golden days!"

Kate nodded in an absent-minded sort of way. She was not taking any of this in. She was here accidentally, as part of chasing a cat and hiding from a coachman, not joining a Rope School. She said, "I must see the captain."

Keane looked doubtful. "He's not an easy man to see," he said. "Not a very kindly man, either. Half Tartar half Turk, actually. Best avoided if possible. They turned him out of his last ship, for excessive cruelty. Maybe in a couple of weeks or so. But only if he's sober and you're lucky. Look here, old Jago'll be after me. You're excused school. First day. Get snugged down, eh? See you later."

He trotted off up the companionway. Kate found she was feeling a fraction less miserable than before. He had tried to cheer her up. He could be a friend.

The Palace was furnished with nothing snugger than a few boxes. She sat down on one of them. It was a sea chest. In the dim light from the horn lantern, she saw that on the lid of the chest in blood-red copperplate it said:

HENRY FORTESCUE

Oh, dear, she thought. So that was it.

She knew that the sons of officers sometimes came with their fathers, to gain a grounding in the sea trade until such time as they were old enough to become midshipmen, the lowest official commissioned rank on one of King George's ships.

So it looked as if the fat man with the broken leg had been Lieutenant Fortescue, on his way to join *Narwhal*. His son Henry would have been ten or eleven years old, come to join the ship as his father's follower, to learn the sea trade. Henry Fortescue had not wanted to learn the sea trade. She remembered the mean white face fleeing through the crowd, the mop of red hair. Hair as red as hers. So now everybody thought she was Master Fortescue, who had a reputation for running away. On a hell ship with a Tartar captain, outward bound for ... months, maybe years.

The sounds of the ship were all around her, full of feet and voices. But she was lonely. She put her face in her hands. Tears ran between the fingers. She was a girl dressed in boy's clothes on a ship where she was not supposed to be, under a name that did not belong to her. At home, Megan would be grousing in the kitchen, and the patients would be writhing in the straps of her uncle's operating chair. The smell of blood would be in the house. Kate hated the smell, and the bellows of pain that crawled under the door from the shop. But just at that moment, she would have given a thousand pounds to be in the parlour above the shop, in her frock and pinny, playing dollies with stupid Sissy from over the road.

The cat came and rubbed itself against her leg, eyeing the parrot in a cage in the corner. Somehow, that made her feel more miserable than ever.

Suddenly, there were tears running down her face. She must go to the captain, Tartar or not, and tell him it was a mistake.

Then she thought, Hold hard, Kate. She had been longing to get away. She had always thought it unfair that girls were not allowed to learn the sea trade. Never mind what girls were not allowed to do, she thought. Accidents had happened, but the results had been fine. What had happened this morning might have looked like a disaster. But viewed another way, it meant that her prayers had been answered.

She thought about that for a moment. The trouble was that as answers to prayers went, it was all a bit sudden and complicated.

Feet clumped on the ladder. The cat skipped away, vanished into the shadows. The clumper was Bryanston. "Blubbing, is it?" he said, his brown face twisted scornfully.

"No," said Kate. Suddenly she felt better. She was angry with the boy for shooting the cat, and angry with herself for sitting there snivelling. She said, "Why do you hate that cat?"

Bryanston said, "Because it's a stupid furry thing and because it belongs to Jago. Jago brought it aboard. Had it in a basket. Jago's a peasant. Stap me, I'm twelve. I should be a midshipman, not a baby in the Rope School. But Mister Jago thinks not, until I can tie a carrick bend with my hands behind me in the dark. Jago's a demmed imposition. I loathe him and I hate his cat. What are you gawping at?"

Kate realized she was indeed staring at him. If Jago had brought the cat aboard *Narwhal* in a basket, how had it come to be tied to Megan's boot scraper with a chewed-off label bearing her name round its neck?

"Babyish," said Bryanston. "That's what it is. And here we are at war with the damned Yankees, in case your peg-leg papa didn't tell you, and we're practicing tying knots, and the ship is swarming with enemy cats. So that's why I hate it."

Kate opened her mouth to tell him that she knew who they were at war with, and that she could not wait for it to stop because her parents—

But Bryanston was bigger than her, and contemplation of Jago's injustices had lit a vicious light in his eye. So she merely said, "What o'clock's dinner?"

"Eight bells," he said. "Oh, I forgot. You're a lubber as well as a blubber. Noon, shore time. Muck it is, too."

Kate's anger straightened her legs. "Where does the captain live?" she said.

"On the quarterdeck," he said. "Why?"

Kate said, "I want to talk to him."

"Ah," said Bryanston. His brown face was suddenly smooth and innocent. "Well, he'll be busy just now. I should just ask Jack Strap if I were you."

"Jack Strap?"

"First   lieutenant.   Second-in-command. Wonderful kindly cove."

Kate went on deck greatly relieved. Keane had

been too timid about her chances of meeting the captain. All she had to do was ask this Mr Strap, and he would take her to the quarterdeck, and she could explain. She knew that by the standards of the giant wooden fortresses of the British Navy, the *Narwhal* was tiny. But after the small, smelly Palace the masts seemed to go all the way up to the sky, and the rail was a frightening distance above the hissing blue sea, and the decks seemed a mile long.

Nonetheless, she squared her shoulders and marched aft, between the knots of sailors, towards the stern of the ship, where a flight of steps led up onto the raised deck where the wheel lived, and underneath which the officers had their cabins.

A man in marine's uniform was standing by the steps. "Please, sir," she said. "I've come to see Jack Strap."

The marine's face twitched. " 'E won't want to see you," he said.

Suddenly there was a face hanging over the rail. It was a red face, with a cocked hat, and sleepless fishskin patches under the eyes, and a long purple nose above a blue uniform jacket much faded by salt and sun. Kate fought a terrible urge to curtsey. "Mr Jack Strap?" she said.

There was a noise like a cannon going off in

39

her face. The brow of the man above her turned black as thunder. "Dam' me!" he roared. "The impertinence of you! Who the blastation are ye, ye imp of Beelzebub?"

Kate said, "If you please, sir, I would see the captain."

"You would, would you?" said the officer. He had a voice like an angry sheep. "Well, the first thing you learn is that my name is Lieutenant Walters, whom you may address as Sir. Not Jack Strap. And the second is that the captain has better things to do than speak to young ragamuffins like you, Master Fortescue. Now, you will do me the favour of climbing to the maintruck."

"The maintruck?" The words did not seem to make sense. Bryanston, she thought. He told me to call the lieutenant by his nickname on purpose.

"Mr Jago!"

Jago trotted aft. "You will explain to Master Fortescue what is the maintruck. And keep him away from the captain, of whom he has some complaint."

Jago's rock-like hand gripped Kate's shoulder. "Fwor," he said, out of the side of his mouth. "You was lucky to get away with your breeches undusted." He pointed up to the middle of the ship's three masts. "See yonder button at the top?"

The button was at the top of the topmost mast. Kate had seen gulls sitting in such places. Her stomach turned over at the thought of going up there herself.

"Here," said Jago. His monkey face looked kindly. "You ain't had no dinner." He pressed something into her hand. "Up you goes, now easy as pie. Look up, is all."

She had questions to ask him. She said, "The cat—"

"Ssh," he said. "Quick, now. Or Jacky Strap'll be arter you."

She nodded. Her mouth was dry. She blinked back the tears. She began to climb.

The first part was almost easy, because she had done it before. After the first platform, the shrouds became narrower. She went up them fast, anger driving her. Unfair, unfair, *unfair*, she thought. That got her to the top of the topmast. Above the topmast was the topgallant mast.

The shrouds up here looked like spiders' webs. The land had moved far away now; the *Narwhal* was corkscrewing over long, low waves. On deck, the motion was a slow heave. Up here, magnified by eighty feet of mast, it was like being on the thin end of a fishing rod.

A bellow floated up from below. Cramping her

41

sore hands on the rope shrouds that made the sides of her ladder, she glanced down.

Below her, the sails stretched like white wings on the yards. It was like being an angel on a church roof, she thought. There were faces upturned down there, watching: Jack Strap, red, and Jago, frowning, as if puzzled. For a moment pleasure and excitement swept through her. She was at sea, aloft. From the position of the sun they were sailing west …

Then her head gave a violent swoop. And she fixed her eyes at the wood of the mast, and concentrated on hanging on for dear life.

More bellowing floated up from the deck. The voice was Jack … Lieutenant Walters'. She knew she had to climb. But her fingers were frozen to the shrouds, and she could not. *Help me*, she thought. *Help me.*

There was a noise above her head. Very slowly, so as not to overbalance, she looked up. Above her was the broad wooden button of the maintruck. Hanging over its side was something fat and furry. The sound came again. "*Braow?*"

My other friend, thought Kate. If you count Keane. Yes, she thought, Keane was all right. Suddenly the fear was gone. Damn Yankee had shown her the way once before. She trusted it to do the same again. She started to climb.

The cat was on the button, breeze ruffling its fur, washing its face. "Morning, Yankee," said Kate. She did not like to say Damn, as it was not a word she had ever used. But Yankee sounded fine; it reminded her of her father.

There was room for both of them on the button. She sat and dangled her feet over eighty feet of empty air, taking care not to look down. The butterflies in her stomach had stopped, and so had the shouting from below.

The cat was warm and furry under her hand. It rubbed its head against her face as if they were already particular friends, which in a manner of speaking they were, what with the cat having landed on the doorstep with its label on, and then having saved Kate's skin on the quay. Kate realized with a shock that it was actually nice up here, suspended in a great blue bowl of sky and sea. Astern, down the white wake of the ship, the Pembroke Dockyard was a grey smudge of smoke at the end of its inlet, growing smaller every second. Here we go, thought Kate. Heading west.

Towards America.

5

Hammock Hook Hitch

The cat sensed that she had lost interest. It stalked away down a tight rope connecting the top of the mainmast with the top of the foremast: the triatic, Kate had heard them call it down at the docks. The wind was growing colder. Kate had no idea when she was allowed down. She began to shiver. She had had nothing to eat since her breakfast bun, six hours ago. She pulled the packet Jago had given her out of her pocket. There was a piece of string, and a small lump of something dark brown that might have been plum cake. When she took a bite, it burned her mouth like fire. "Ugh," she cried, spitting. "Tobacco!"

She was hungry, she was lonely, and she was frightened. She started to cry. Something warm and furry rubbed against her leg. The cat was back.

"Yank," she said.

The cat sniffed at the fingers that still held the plug of chewing tobacco. Delicately, it took it in its teeth, and trotted off down the taut rope.

She forgot to cry. She stared after it with her mouth open. "Dratted animal," said a voice below her.

She peered gingerly down. It was the mean-faced Bryanston, running up the ratlines with the agility of a spider, scarcely touching the ropes with his hands. "Budge up," he said, shoving his way on to the button so he nearly pushed her off. His face twisted into an elaborately sweet smile. "Jago taught it to chew. Jago can teach anyone to do anything." He pulled out a short pipe and lit it with the professional air becoming one who would shortly be a midshipman, coughing only slightly. "Jack Strap says you can come down now. And if he has the like again, he'll see you on mouse day."

Kate said, "Why did you do that?"

Bryanston said, "Teach you your place, brat."

Kate was about to argue. But he was bigger than her, and they were eighty feet in the air, and he was a swine. So instead she said, "What's mouse day?"

He grinned an unkind grin. "Mondays," he said. "When you meet the ship's cat. Not the one you met. The other one, with nine tails."

"But I must see the captain."

Bryanston pointed to the stern of the ship, where a tiny figure in a cocked hat was peering through a telescope at the arms of a semaphore on a distant headland. "That's him," he said. "So you've seen him. But you're a bad lad now, because you cheeked our Jacky. Bad lads like you, this is as close as you get, if you've got any sense."

He looked at her sideways. He had hard black eyes. Just at that moment, they looked as if they were adding Kate up, and not arriving at the right total. "Jacky sent me to get you down," said Bryanston. "Dinner time."

Cautiously, Kate swung her legs over the edge of the button and started the endless journey to the deck. She could not see Jago anywhere.

They gave her beef stew and bread baked in Pembroke and already going stale. There were four others in the mess: Bryanston, and Keane, and the pint-sized Bean brothers. They talked about things Kate scarcely understood. But listening to them, she began to get excited.

The parrot in the Palace was called Cudjoe. Keane said they had picked him up when they had been hunting slave ships off the Fever Coast. He spoke with thrilling familiarity of the Coast, whose king sat on a throne of skulls and had a bodyguard of huge, murderous women. Tormented by Bryanston, the parrot became agitated and swore terribly. On the Coast, they said, they had had a monkey that swung in the rigging, gibbering. The monkey had looked exactly like Jago. The conversation drifted on to Jago. Bryanston scowled, and opined that he was up to no good. The smaller Bean brother said Jago knew how to make a bunny out of string. The bigger Bean brother hit the smaller Bean brother for being pathetic. Bryanston laughed. Keane separated them with good humour, winking at Kate.

Then all of them except Bryanston went and played a form of tag in the rigging. When she looked up, from the foretop, Kate saw Jago high up the mainmast on the roayl yard, his ape's silhouette black against the sky, pigtail lashing in the breeze, gazing at the horizon. She wanted to ask him about what Bryanston had said about the cat, but she could not persuade herself to climb all that way. Once, she found his eye resting upon her. She thought that when she stared back, he looked away too quickly.

But there was not much time for wondering why, because the boys were a rowdy lot, and in the absence of Bryanston, Kate found them such good company that she forgot about her bundle of clothes above the smithy in Pembroke Dock, and almost started to believe she was Master Fortescue.

The sun fell towards the horizon dead ahead. Still west, thought Kate. She tried to think of her parents, miles beyond the horizon. But thinking of them was uncomfortable, because it made her think of the past and the future, and things she would like to change that could never be changed. So she locked it away with some difficulty in her mind, and buried it in the same place as the dream.

The dream was always the same, and Kate did not have to be asleep to dream it. There was a wood, with trees growing out of clear, shiny water. On an island in the wood stood a log cabin. In front of the log cabin sat a man smoking a pipe with two copper-coloured Indians who were wearing eagle feathers and long robes like dressing-gowns, with gold braid at wrist and hem. The man with the pipe was her father. He had red hair and green eyes. There was a woman beside him, plucking a turkey the size of a pig. The woman was her mother, and she had shot the turkey that morning. Inside the log cabin was nearly enough money to send for Kate across the Atlantic, but not quite—

"Coming!" yelled the elder Bean, swinging like an ape from the foremast to the mainyard.

At eight bells, Jago rounded up the boys and drove them below. "Bedtime, me lovelies," he said.

Kate hung back, to get him to herself. She said, "What about the cat?"

Jago gazed at her with eyes lit innocent blue by the evening sun. "Cat?" he said.

"Someone left the cat on my doorstep. Your cat. With a note. It scrabbled up the note, but I could read my name."

"Good gosh," said Jago. "Zat right, izzit? Must of bin stole."

"But it's yours—"

"Robbers and willans," said Jago. "Festering with the brutes, ashore. You wants straight talk and precision of rectitude, you comes to sea. Like as what you 've done, my anzum. 'Urry upalong, now." And he hustled her below.

Kate stood looking nervously at the wooden walls of the Palace. It was too small for beds.

Jago was looking at her. " 'Ammocks," he said. "We uses 'ammocks, my anzum."

The boys were already working at rolls of white canvas slung along the walls. In a matter of seconds, they had unrolled all except one, and climbed in, still wearing their shirts and breeches. Dirty, thought Kate. But she was relieved that nobody had

had to undress. That had been another worry …

Another thing to push into the locked room in her mind. "Go on," said Jago. "That's yours."

Awkwardly, Kate unrolled the sausage of stiff canvas.

"Lookee year," said Jago, catching hold of the hook at one end. "You'll make this 'ere fast with the 'ammock 'ook 'itch."

Kate said, "With the what?"

Jago unfurled the canvas sausage into a flat sheet, pulled a cord from a hook on the bulkhead. His fingers moved with dazzling speed. The hammock was suddenly tied. "Arright?" he said. "Now you do him, Master Fortescue."

He untied the knot with a flick of his fingers. It was dark, and Kate had not seen what he had done. But she did not like to admit defeat. So she made the best knot she could, and stared at him defiantly.

He stared back, the yellow lamp gleaming in the slits of his eyes. "Wery good," he said. "Now you climb aboard, my lad. Arse first, then turn yerself sidewise."

Kate sat in the hammock, rolled in. The hammocks were close as pilchards in a barrel. The smaller Bean had a teddy bear made out of rope.

Keane was next to her. She whispered, "Where are we going?"

"Nowhere," said Keane. "Which is to say, west, beyond the Isles of the jolly old Blest, because a Yankee privateer's out there, somewhere. We're looking for him. If you see him, raise your angel voice and Capn'll give you a guinea." Kate could see it in her head: a coin red-gold as a setting sun.

"Which it is etiquette to share with your mates," said Bryanston, with a hideous leer.

"Shut up," said Keane.

Kate's eyelids felt heavy as lead. Sleep covered her …

Something banged her on the head, hard. She yelled. She was on a hard wooden deck. A figure was standing over her in the lamplight.

"Lesson one," said Jago's hoarse voice from the shadows. "When you ties a knot, lives will depend on 'im. So if you don't understand 'im, ast me agin. I don't bite."

Kate was furious, the way you are furious when you hit your head. She was not going to cry. "Show me again," she said. Bryanston was watching her. She avoided his eye.

Jago lifted the lantern and showed her. She tried again. That time, she got it right. "Good boy," said Jago. "Slippery 'itches is trouble, nothing but." Kate thought of the runaway carriage. Too true, she thought. "Now you climb aboard and sleep tight." He put his face so close to hers that she could smell the tar on his pigtail, and dropped his voice to a hoarse whisper. "And tomorrow, or the next day, or the day after that, we shall see."

Kate lay as rigid as it is possible to lie in a hammock. See what? Had he found out that she was an impostor? If so, why would he be keeping quiet about it? There was so much stuff in the locked room in her mind that she thought her head would explode.

A voice beside her said, "You all right?" Keane's voice.

Her head felt suddenly better. Sympathy brought a lump to her throat. "Fine," she said.

Bryanston said, "Lubber!"

"Suddenly the air is filled with plaguey miasmas," said Keane.

"Watch your lip, young 'un," said Bryanston, low and evil.

Keane shut up.

This time, Kate did not sleep. She lay in the thick dark and listened to the regular stretch and groan of the ship's timbers. Her head was hurting. She thought of her garret, the moon riding outside the diamond panes of her window. She thought of Jack … Lieutenant Walters and Bryanston, and what Jago had said about tomorrow. She felt suddenly frightened. She wanted to know what was happening to her, even if it was horrible. She wanted to get back.

But with Jack Strap and the marine standing guard over the quarterdeck, there was only one way to get back: up the shrouds and over the triatic, the tightrope eighty empty feet above the deck that connected the top of the mainmast with the top of the mizzen; then down the shrouds to the quarterdeck, beard the Tartar captain, tell the truth—

Each stage of it was more impossible than the last. And what would happen when she did get back would be the worst of the lot. It made her feel sick just thinking about it.

Perhaps Jago had the answer. But if he did not want to talk about it, it would make no difference whether he had it or not.

6

Rope School

She was still feeling sick when she awoke, but for different reasons. Bryanston was standing by her hammock, shoving her arm. "Breakfast," he said. "Pump's on deck."

Head swimming, she stumbled up the steep steps, out of the stuffy reek of the Palace and into the fresh air.

The air was almost too fresh. A heavy breeze was tearing across the deck loaded with salt spray. She lurched to the pump, pulled the handle a couple of times and splashed water on her face. Up above a corduroy of lead-coloured cloud was lumbering down the sky. The sea was full of marching grey hills of water, armed with dirty white teeth of foam.

Yesterday's mass of canvas had vanished. Now there were only a couple of thin strips of sail, stretched cracking-tight against the clouds. The mast jerked against the sky like an angry man's walking stick.

The pump water was cold. Kate started to shiver, and could not stop. She ran below. The Palace seemed full of boys tricing up hammocks. Keane beckoned her over with his eyes, and showed her the knots. Now, she watched closely, and got it right first time, despite her queasiness.

"Clever," said Bryanston, who had been watching her hard from a distance. Much to her relief, she could detect no meanness in his face. "I'll get ye some breakfast. Sling us the kid, Shrimp!"

They had lowered a table from the ceiling. The smaller Bean handed him a covered cooking pot. Five minutes later, Brayanston was back, with a bag of biscuits, and something in the pot that smelled of fat.

"Budge up," said Bryanston. He sat down beside Kate, elbowing Keane out of the way. "Hardtack, now," he said. "Old hardtack, too. Pusser and Cap'n lining their pockets at the expense of poor sailormen. Lookee here." He took one of the biscuits. It was two inches thick, six inches square, pricked with little holes. "Bang 'im on the table," he said.

Kate banged. A dozen little beetles fell out of the

holes and scuttled away into the darkness.

"Weevils," said Bryanston. The ship lurched and the lamp swung. Kate watched him, horrified, as he dabbed one up on his finger and ate it. "Nasty bitter taste."

The ship lurched again. Kate found she did not feel like having a biscuit. Most particularly, she did not feel like having a biscuit full of weevils.

"Don't fancy it?" said Bryanston, elaborately surprised. "Try a nice bit of fat bacon, then?" He wagged a greasy lump of rind under her nose.

Kate looked full into his dirty, sallow face. She could see the meanness now. She could not imagine how she had missed it. "Thank you, no," she said.

His sarcastic laughter followed her as she ran up to the deck and was sick over the rail. He was still laughing when she came below.

She sat on a sea-chest. Bryanston said, "Strap told Jago you was to be in the Rope School today."

Kate could not remember feeling more ill. But at eight bells, she dragged herself up the companionway, into the wind-moaning main-shrouds, and up to the big platform of the maintop.

The others were already there, Jago in the middle of the circle. Jago winked, said something about a knot. "Lookee here," he said, holding up a piece of rope.

His fingers moved. He tied a knot, quickly. "Now you," he said.

Kate turned away, stuck her head over the edge of the platform. There were a lot of sailors on deck, far below. One of them was wearing a red bobble hat. She was sick on the bobble hat. There was a roar of rage, laughter and applause.

Jago said, "Oo, dear. Like that, eh? Mr Keane, you will kindly see Mr Fortescue right."

Keane took her back to the Palace and helped to sling her hammock. A sailor gave her some medicine that sent her to sleep.

She lay there for two days. On the third day, she felt better, and rolled out of her hammock. She felt light and thin, as if the daylight would shine right through her. She could have done with a bowl of broth and a new loaf from Mrs Jones the bakery.

Bryanston's lower lip was sticking out. He said, "It's your day for the galley run, but they made me do it." He glared across at Keane, and plonked down a biscuit and the kid of salt pork.

This time, she was ravenous. The biscuit was like a stone, and the pork was stringy. But Keane showed her how to get rid of the weevils, and soften up the biscuit in the pork juice. She found that if she shut her eyes, she could imagine she was at home, eating the fag-ends of bacon and stale crusts that Megan told her she was lucky to get. She was surprised to find that this food tasted rather better.

"Now," said Bryanston. "Jago told me to show you the ship." He did not look pleased. "Come on."

"Can't Keane?" said Kate.

"Orders," said Bryanston.

They squeezed among the crowds of sailors on the upper decks, down to the bottom of the companionway, the central staircase that ran from top to bottom of the sloop's three decks. It was pitch black down there. There were no other people, and it stank. "You get bad air," Bryanston said from the darkness somewhere in front of her. "People die."

"Oh," said Kate, squinting in the general direction of the voice. The other voices of the ship seemed far away.

"Slowly," he said, and laughed a hollow laugh. "She's a captured ship. When she was a Frenchie, they used to bury the dead down here. Under your feet. Dirty beggars."

The hull creaked. Water sloshed. There was gravel underfoot.

"The bilges," he said. The crunch of his feet on the gravel quickened. He was running. Panic surged up in Kate. She ran after him, through darkness like a lake of ink. Her head slammed into something hard: a pile of barrels. The stink was awful. *Bad air. People die.* The panic got worse. She lay there. *So this is it*, she thought.

Something furry brushed against her face. *"Braow?"* said a small voice. Yank, she thought. To the rescue. All you need is one friend. Someone did care, after all. And she could breathe.

She scrambled on to her hands and knees. She found a way round the barrels, splashed through filthy water, scrambled over a pile of boxes. There was a patch of light ahead, dim and yellow. Against the light she saw Yank, tail up like a flag. She fell flat on her face in stinking water. She thought, *Saved.* She crawled on, almost cheerfully.

Bryanston was sitting on the hatch, kicking his legs. "Thought you'd never come," he said.

Kate pushed past him. The light above the hatch must have been dim, but after the darkness of the bilges it was bright enough to make her screw up her eyes. Her clothes were soaked with filthy water. She wanted to be sick, but she was not going to be sick in front of Bryanston. "Very interesting, I found that," she said. "And where are we now?"

He looked taken aback. Kate's sickness faded, giving ground to triumph. "Gun deck," he said.

It was a long, wooden room. Cannons were

lashed to the deck, facing their gun ports. In a battle, the gun ports would be opened, the guns run out so their muzzles stuck through the sides of the ship. Kate had read the ballads they sold in the streets, knew about "Hearts of Oak", "The Cannon's Roar". It surprised her how peaceful it all looked, and how terribly it smelled of old smoke, and lavatories, and bilge.

"Can't take you to the captain," said Bryanston, smirking, and jerking his thumb at the wooden wall separating the back end of the ship from the gun deck. "But I'll show you the heads."

Kate had already found the heads, the ship's lavatories, perched under the beak of the bows. She did not particularly want to see them again. But Bryanston gripped her arm and shoved her through the throngs of sailors along the gun-deck to the smelly little room where the white foam of the bow-wave piled under the hole in the deck. "Lovely, isn't it?" he said. Then he grabbed the back of her neck, and tried to shove her head into the seat.

Kate had had enough. She kicked him in the shin, hard. He jumped back. His fist came out and banged her on the ear. It hurt. She whacked at him blindly.

"Oh," said Bryanston. "Slappy slappies. Fights like a girl, does it?"

Kate's anger increased. She bunched up her fist and planted it smack in the middle of his smirking face.

The smirk disappeared. He advanced. None of the sailors so much as looked round.

Things walloped Kate from all sides. She fell onto the deck. Her ears were ringing. Bryanston landed heavily on her, knees on her shoulders. His face was red and blotchy, shiny with rage. "You just remember who's cock of the Palace, eh? No good you coming the brave runaway. You're a milk-and-watery one, Fortescue. And from now, you do what I says, and you see the captain when I says, and you don't speak unless spoken to."

"Hey," said a voice. It was high, trembling a little with the knowledge of its own bravery. Keane's voice. "Leave him alone."

Bryanston got up. He towered over Keane. "What business is it of yours?" he said.

Keane's voice became more confident. "You're a bully, sir. Tyrant and oppressor—"

Bryanston pushed him hard in the chest.

Keane lurched backwards into a cannon, bouncing off a sailor hanging washing on a line between the guns. The sailor grinned, but made no move to stop the flight.

"Come on, then," said Bryanston.

Blood was running from Keane's nose. Kate thought, Maybe if we both go for him—

Somewhere in the ship a bell rang eight times.

"Blast," said Bryanston. "Rope School. I'll kill you. Later."

He trotted aft, weaving between the sailors.

Kate put her hand on Keane's shoulder. She said, "Thank you. Are you all right?"

"Course," said Keane, scrubbing at his nose with his sleeve. "Sorry. Should have warned you about Bryanston."

Kate said, "It's not your fault."

Keane looked round at her. There was blood smeared over his upper lip, but he was grinning. It was a friendly grin. "We likes to look after our friends," he said, highly piratical. "Being as how we don't have no mothers or fathers to do the looking out for us, like. Being all in the same boat, in a manner of speaking." Then in his normal voice he said, "You'll need some line."

She said, "Where do I find that?"

"Ask him," said Keane, pointing at a sailor who had just finished carving himself a chew of tobacco.

The sailor said, "Here," and handed her a length of thinnish cord. She rolled it up and stuffed it in her pocket, and ran up the companionway.

After the piebald darkness of the gun deck, the daylight was dazzling in the maintop, the platform where Kate had fallen asleep when she had first arrived on the *Narwhal*. She went up the shrouds like a squirrel. She told herself that less than a week ago, she had been on dry land. But she did not really believe it.

As she came over the edge of the maintop she found the followers were aloft, perched in a circle like crows in a nest, Jago in the middle.

"That's better," said Jago to Kate. His eyes were bright and knowing on her bruised face.

The ship rolled. She grabbed a rope to stop herself falling, and looked down at the tiny deck, far below.

"One 'and for yerself, and the other for the ship," said Jago. "Now, then. What one of you can tie Jago a bowline?"

7

Footrope Knot

Opposite Kate, Bryanston's fingers became a blur of speed. She looked over his shoulder. Then she pulled her bit of cord from her pocket and began to twist it.

Bryanston finished the knot. He looked across and smirked scornfully.

Jago said, "Tell unto Master Fortescue the purpose of the bowline."

Bryanston chanted in a high, sarcastic voice. "The-purpose-of-the-bowline-is-to-create-a-loop-that-will-not-slip-nor-capsize-while-remaining-easy-to-untie."

"Correck," said Jago.

Bryanston held out the rope, made a loop, tied the knot as fast as he possibly could. Kate followed his movements with furious concentration. Then she tied the knot. Bryanston clapped sarcastically.

The Bean brothers, who had been watching him anxiously, followed his lead. Keane winked.

"Again," said Jago. "The lot of you." Kate tied the knot. Then she tied it five times more. Then she tied it behind her back, and with her eyes shut.

"All right," said Jago. "Now, the sheet bend."

They spent the rest of the morning up there, tying knots. At the end of the session, Jago said, "Yardarms. You're a light one, Mr Fortescue. We'll have you on the royal yard. That's the one right at the top. I'll look arter ye."

The royal yard looked the size of a matchstick as Kate started up the topmast shrouds. Her legs were shaking. She could feel Jago's weight stretching the ropes below. He called out a running commentary. "So hup we goes," he said. "And arter the main yard we has the topsail yard. And so *hon*, climb up the houtside shrouds 'ere known as the futtock shrouds, not through the 'ole in the middle known as the lubber's 'ole." Kate found herself climbing a sort of rope ladder that hung outwards, two houses high above the deck. The bruises hurt. She felt weak after her seasickness. Through a dry throat, she told herself, *You will not cry*. The breath came in big, rasping sobs that hurt her chest. But always Jago, below, drove her on with his cheerful commentary. "So arter the topsails we 'as the topgallants, and arter the topgallants we 'as the royals. Which, as you will obserwe, is thin and delicate, as yards go, so we sends up 'ere only the lightest and most gazellish of our people, including today yourself and myself …"

Kate was hardly listening. She was hoping a lot of things. She was hoping that Jago would not conclude that the bruises on her face had been caused by the fists of Bryanston, because if he did, and Bryanston got into trouble, Bryanston would get cross, the way Megan got cross on the one occasion when Uncle Owen had tried in his hesitant way to chide her for maltreating Kate.

Kate was surprised to find that thinking of Megan was like looking down the wrong end of a telescope. The memory came with a smell, of course: Auntie's shift, which she did not change very often, and the flat stink of heavy rubbish bins in the back scullery—

"Right you are," said Jago's voice, below. "To the yardarm, my boy."

The yardarm was the outside end of the yard. She looked out to a fat, horizontal pole along the top of the sail. A rope was slung underneath it in a loop.

"Footrope," said Jago. "You leans your belly on the yard, and you folds yourself up like a clarps knife, and you walks sidewise like a Hector crab, leaving the flippers free. Like this 'ere." He stepped sideways onto the sagging footrope, leaned his stomach on the spar, and walked outwards, towards the end of the yard. "Lookee," he said, waving his long, tattooed arms. "Hands free, for making what means letting out, or furling, what means rolling up sail. Come along now."

He could have been born balancing on a rope, Kate thought. The salt wind was buffeting her face. Jago's sea-blue eyes were gleaming. There was something tough and urgent about him. More urgent, she suddenly thought, than simple curiosity to see how a new pupil would behave up here on the royal yard.

Suddenly she was very frightened and very curious.

"Come you *hon*," said Jago.

She swallowed nothing, and shuffled out along the footrope, leaning forward the way she had seen the men lean forward when they were making sail.

Keane was on another yard, below her. Down there she could hear the boys yelling like sparrows. Her mouth was too dry to yell.

So she shuffled instead.

The rope under her feet was as tight as a rail. She

found that as long as her weight was on the spar, she could stand firm. She began to feel almost confident.

Jago was waiting at the end, the yardarm. Kate felt triumphant as a perching bird. She was grinning so hard her face wanted to come in half. She said, "It's easy."

He grinned, a monkey grin that showed his blood-red gums. "Fair weather," he said. "You try a-doing of it on the Grand Banks of Newfoundland when the salt water's coming across of you green, a-freezing as it comes, and the canvas feels like Swansea tin plate, if you could feel it at all, but you haven't felt foot nor finger since four bells, it now being eight." He pulled a little pewter box out of his breeches. "Easy as pie," he said. "Still and all, you got up here, Master … Fortescue." He was watching her too closely with his sky-blue eyes. He left just enough hesitation in front of the name for Kate's stomach to turn over. He must have forgotten it, she told herself. "So welcome to the Rope School."

She still felt ridiculously pleased with herself. She nearly curtseyed, but luckily it is not easy to curtsey when you are standing no-hands on the footrope of a royal yard some eighty feet above the deck of one of His Majesty's sloops of war.

From the pewter box Jago took a long black pigtail of tobacco. He opened his clasp knife, cut off a quid, shoved it into his cheek, and spat down to leeward. Kate leaned on the spar. It was pleasant up here in the breeze. She was only Kate Griffiths, led astray by a mysterious cat. But she had got herself into the Rope School. Megan, you bat, she thought. If only you could see me now.

She noticed a curious thing.

Jago had not put the tobacco box back in his pocket. The sun was out, gleaming on the blue sea, and the white sails, and the varnished wood of the spar, and the gold earring in his ear.

And the bottom of the tobacco box.

It lit the bottom of the box because Jago was holding it between his hard brown fingers, and turning the box so that the sun slanted across it. And the bottom of the box was polished to such a high sheen that it reflected the sun like the looking-glass Kate had once used to direct a piercing ray of light into the closet of Pastor Meredith when Pastor Meredith had been kissing Dilys, his maid.

Kate was transfixed.

Jago's attention had left her. He was concentrating on aiming a beam of light across the blue waves to the empty horizon.

Kate stared at that horizon as if at any moment

a scroll of words would rise from the sea and explain to her all mysteries, like a scroll she dimly remembered in the Book of Revelation.

But of course there was no scroll, only the empty western horizon.

The not quite empty western horizon.

Far out there on the knife-cut rim of the world, a tiny sun winked and died, winked and died again.

Kate said, "What—"

Jago turned. "Breathe a word," he said. "One word. And I'll kill ye. Keep quiet, and you'll thank me for it." He stuffed the pewter box back in his pocket. He was not smiling, and his blue eyes were as hot as a well-blown forge. He looked capable of killing. "You saw nothing," he said.

Kate could not meet the eyes. She looked down to the little leaf of wood that was *Narwhal's* deck. She remembered what Keane had told her. *There's a Yankee privateer out there, somewhere.*

And Jago had been signalling.

She looked down. Below her, the sail was a hard white curve of wind-filled canvas. Below the sail was a tiny red face, attached to a tiny blue coat. Lieutenant Walters.

The triumph had gone. Her belly was cold as ice. Her thoughts tolled like a bell. Jago behaved something like a friend, but he might be a traitor. And I have seen him signalling, and he may kill me if I tell anyone, but how will I be able not to do my duty and tell Lieutenant Walters everything, as soon as he asks?

Her knees were water. She clung to something, she did not know what it was. The sea stretched blue as a sapphire to the western horizon. Empty—

The footrope jerked under her feet. The jerk threw her off balance. She stood up straight, forgetting to rest her stomach on the yard. Her fingers scrabbled at the yard, but the yard was a fat pole of smooth, varnished wood, without handholds. Her mouth was open. She was screaming, a scream of pure terror. The ship rolled, heaving the yard like an animal shaking itself free of a burden. She fell backwards into space.

8

Telescope Splice

She thought about the cat. Cat, she thought, you led me to sanctuary aboard the *Narwhal*. But now, at the end of it, on the hard deck, something too horrible to think about is going to happen, so I will never see my mother and father or even Uncle Owen or even Aunt Megan again, and it is going to happen *now*.

As she thought *now* her shoulders slammed into something hard, and she screamed.

But she was still falling.

Not so much falling as sliding, fast, down a great white slope.

Down the topsail.

A bit of rope lashed her hand. She grabbed at it. It burned her, whipped away. She yelled a despairing yell. She slid off the edge of the sail, into space.

Someone was shouting far below, down there on

the deck. She fell another five feet …

Into a hammock.

Except that it was not a hammock. It was a bag of stiff white canvas, loosely gathered. It was the mainsail, furled along the main yard. She lay. A sailor's face appeared in the crack of sky at its top. She did not know the sailor. A voice said, "Blow me down. You alive in there?"

Kate checked, gingerly. "I think so," she said. A tattooed arm reached down for her. She pulled herself up, out of the salty canvas smell of the sail, and into the wind.

She moved as if in a trance. Later, she could never remember how she got back to the deck.

All she knew was that it felt wonderfully solid. As she jumped out of the shrouds, her knees gave way. She sat on the deck, hard, and started to shake. I will not cry, she thought. But the tears went running down her face anyway.

A shadow fell on her. "Well, now," said the edgy snarl of Lieutenant Walters. "It's the lubberly Master Fortescue, a-learning how to fly."

She tried to smile. It was not a success.

"Hup with you," he said. "Come hup, I say."

She managed to stand.

"Now," he said. There was a smile on his meaty red face. It reminded her of Bryanston's smile.

"You will do me the honour of climbing to the maintruck."

She gaped at him.

"Mustn't let yer confidence blow away, must we?" he said, quietly. The veins in his neck suddenly bulged like thick ropes. "HOP TO IT!" he roared.

The tears blurred her vision.

"LEAP, you lubberly insect!" yelled Walters. "HUP! I say, or I'll tan yer hide on mouse day."

Kate looked round. Keane was standing on deck, straight as a ramrod. He winked at her.

Kate winked back. A new feeling washed over her. All her life, she had been lonely. Now she had a real friend.

She climbed.

And she realized that Jack Strap had been right. Her confidence had not had time to blow away. She felt absolutely no fear. It was as if the ship had done what it could to her, and failed to beat her, and she had beaten it. She climbed to the maintop, and up the topmast, and up the topgallant mast past the royal yard where she had fallen. The sea was a mazy roar far below, the wind a big cool hand pressing her into the safe web of the rigging. She went to the button on top of the mast and sat there with her feet propped on the triatic.

Damn Yankee came and sat with her, dribbling tobacco juice on her breeches. She wished he could talk. Down on the quarterdeck the captain paced, his jacket sapphire-blue in the sun. The triatic stretched across to the top of the mizzen mast like a tightrope. *Dare I?* thought Kate.

But even if she got across the triatic, she did not know what she would tell him. It had been complicated enough before Jago. Now the horizon had winked back at his tobacco box.

Jago, who had been kind.

If she stood in front of the captain, she would not be able to stop herself telling him everything. Jago might be a traitor, and hang for it. Or, she might not be believed, and Jago would do something dreadful to her. And she would never find out what he meant when he'd said, *Keep quiet, and you'll thank me for it.*

It was all very confusing. But there was one part of it that was straightforward.

No captain. She pulled her mind away, gazed out at the glittering bowl of the sea, the horizon an unbroken line around her.

A not quite unbroken line.

Far to the west, a whisker of something no bigger than a single eyelash cut the smooth edge of the world. It was so tiny that when Kate looked straight at it, it disappeared. But when she looked to one side of it, she saw it for what it was: the mast of a ship, so distant that her hull was hidden by the curve of the earth, and only the slender spar of her main topmast showed.

Kate had spent a lot of her life watching ships. English sailing ships had sails made of white cotton canvas brought from the distant, hot reaches of the Empire. Their sails were often yellow-cream, made in the cold northern states from unbleached flax.

As Kate watched, the ship over the horizon set a minute dot of sail.

The dot was yellowish cream.

She remembered what Keane had told her in the Palace, her first night. *Sing out, and Cap'n'll give you a guinea!*

"Ship!" she yelled. Her voice was a mouse-like squeak in the roar of the wind. "Ship AHOOOY!"

Nobody on deck looked up. But someone in the shrouds below did. Bryanston.

He had heard. His face was tight and cunning. She knew what he was going to do. Desperation squeezed at her heart. She shouted again, "Ship *ahoy!*"

Bryanston shouted. He shouted as if his lungs were made of leather. Far below on the quarterdeck, the captain's dark head of hair turned into a little brown circle, uplifted.

"Ship *ahoy!*" howled Bryanston again.

"A guinea for that lad!" roared a deep voice from the quarterdeck. "Hands make sail!"

And suddenly, like a tree packed with roosting starlings, the rigging was full of men.

Kate sat above it all. She watched as the men took off the white topgallant and bent on a yellow one. "One of the sails she 'ad when she was a Frenchie," said one of them. "So he'll think we're friendly until we're right on him. I should go down now." Kate nodded dumbly.

Over the horizon, the tiny masts had grown.

Heavy rumbling came up through the timber of the mast. Her skin crawled as if someone had dropped a key down her back.

The ports in the ship's side were open now. Sweating and cursing at the tackles, *Narwhal's* crew were running out the guns.

She slid down the shrouds to the deck. The *Narwhal* had every shred of sail set. She was leaning far over to starboard, pounding across the deep blue waves like a cheetah pursuing a gazelle.

Jack Strap saw her running. He roared, "Avast there!" She skidded to a halt. "What're you at on deck?" he said, the blood purpling his beefy jowls. "Get up there to the royal yard."

Jago was suddenly at her side. "First voyage,

Mr Walters," he said, "I reckon … Ah!" His long, tattooed arm uncoiled and seized somebody who was slinking towards the main companionway. "Mr Bryanston's a good man for the royal yard, beggin' your pardon, sir."

Jack Strap's eyes rolled ponderously between Bryanston and Kate. He grunted. "Ye have a point, schoolmaster," he said. "Up, Bryanston. Fortescue, dam'-yer-eyes, make yourself useful. See to it, schoolmaster."

"Aye, aye, *zur*," said Jago.

Bryanston directed a look of pure hatred at Kate. He said, quietly, "I'll get you for this."

Jago said, "You 'eard the hofficer, Mr Bryanston."

Slowly and unwillingly, Bryanston swung into the shrouds and began to climb.

"Bit 'ot, up aloft, in action," said Jago cheerfully to Kate. "Now you get below and lend a hand." His eyes were glittering as ever. But Kate, looking into them, thought she could see something new there. It could not have been fear, so it must have been worry, as if something he had hoped would work out one way was working out another. He said, "That was you saw him first, eh?"

She nodded. She was not really sure how he would take it. But she was not going to hide the fact that she was proud of herself. Fourth day at sea, disguised as a boy, and it was she that had sighted the Yankee privateer.

Jago said, "I'll tell Strap. You'll get your guinea."

She was hardly bothered about the guinea. She said, "Will we catch him?"

He looked at her solemnly with his brilliant eyes. Then he grinned, the grin that showed his blood-red gums. "Chip off the old block," he said. "*Hif* ever I seed one."

Yank was rubbing against her leg. "What do you mean?" she said.

He laughed. He said, "Best see Cookie, get some prog for the mog. Then get back to the Palace." He loped away, uncoiled an arm, swung himself into the shrouds and melted into the spider's web of the rigging.

One of these days, thought Kate. One of these days, after the battle, if there is to be a battle, I will find a way to make you explain.

Kate went to the galley, where Cookie was dousing the stoves in case a shot scattered hot ashes through the ship. She found some mackerel for Yank, who ate it and slid away goodness knew where. She felt foreign and useless among the hurrying men. There was a new feeling in the ship. It was the feeling that ran through Uncle Owen's shop as he unpacked his horrible instruments before a difficult operation: partly excitement, and partly a very grown-up sort of determination. It was a feeling that in Kate's mind came before bellows of pain from inside the locked door of the shop. The excitement dimmed. She walked slowly below.

Sand had been scattered on the gun deck. A couple of boys were wetting it down with the canvas hose of the ship's pump. Kate had heard about that, down in the dockyards. The idea was to put out any stray sparks before they could catch the wooden fabric of the ship. The elder Bean was staggering up from the Palace, carrying two bundles of rolled up canvas. "Come on," he piped. "All hammocks on deck."

Kate went into the Palace, untied the hammock hook hitch with fingers that seemed even clumsier than usual, and carried the stiff canvas sausage up into the light.

The American's sails were visible from the deck now. When Kate looked up, she saw that the *Narwhal* was flying the French tricolour from her mizzen mast.

Jago was on deck again. He grinned at her. She still thought he looked worried, but he was in too much of a hurry for her to tell. "Now you lash that

80

there 'ammock along the rail, using the parallel 'itch as I showed you this forenoon."

"What for?"

"Stops bullets," said Jago. "If so be as you be lucky. Then you get yourself below, boy, and keep out of 'arm's way."

The *Narwhal's* bow crashed into a wave, and spray spattered down her deck, soaking the tight-lashed hammocks. Kate started for the hatch. Then she paused.

The privateer was not more than a mile away, and the gap between the two ships was closing fast. She was a three-masted schooner, longer than the *Narwhal*. A big Stars and Stripes streamed from her gaff peak. Even at this distance, the sails looked stretched and baggy, the ship's paint streaked and flaking. She was a long way from home, and she had been at sea for a long time.

A seaman at a gun said, "Come on, yew beauty."

Battles meant prize money, when you beat your enemy and took his ship back into harbour. The thought of it ran though the *Narwhal* like a fire down a train of gunpowder. Suddenly Kate was violently excited, more excited than she had ever been.

A line of flags had broken open at the privateer's

yardarm and fluttered stiff as boards in the breeze. Signal flags, thought Kate, straining her eyes. But they were only coloured dots against the sky. They made no sense to her. The silence deepened.

"Recognition signal," said the sailor at the gun. "Cap'n'll have to answer. Or else."

The officers put their heads together on the quarterdeck. Someone barked an order. A hoist of flags soared to *Narwhal's* yardarm, snapped open. There was a moment in which even the sea seemed to hold its breath.

Then Kate heard a flurry of shouting from the privateer. Her rigging was suddenly alive with men, and the canvas blossomed from her topsail yards like snow-patches on the Presely hills.

"Rumbled us, be God!" roared the voice of Lieutenant Walters. "Fire!"

9

Gunner's Knot

There was a bang that seemed to drive Kate's eardrums together in the middle of her head, and the *Narwhal*'s hull shook. White tree-trunks of water blossomed round the gilded carving of the American ship's stern as the recoil drove the guns back in their tackles. The *Narwhal* wheeled until her bowsprit was pointing downwind, at the American's stern. A white ensign rose to her spanker gaff peak, fluttering and stiffening in the wind.

"Stern chase, is it?" said one of the gun's crews.

"What?" said Kate, out of a throat dry with fear and sulphur.

"He's off downwind," said the man. "Away from us, so as we can't point a gun at 'im, on account of most of our guns faces sidewise, like. So we'll have to catch 'im and pull up alongside of 'im afore we can give 'im the weight of our broadside. And 'e reckons 'e'll be too farst for we."

"Oh," said Kate. Her ears were humming, and her insides felt loose at their moorings. She was surprised at the disappointment that flooded through her.

The first sailor rammed home a bag of powder, a cloth wad and a cannonball. He spat tobacco-juice into the blue water racing past the *Narwhal's* side. The man who had aimed the gun said, " 'E be wrong."

"Wrong?"

"*Narwhal's* farster nor him," said the aimer. "Used to be the fastest ship in the Frenchie fleet. Wait and see." He was as calm as if they were betting which gull would flap off a post first.

Kate waited, taking deep breaths and holding them, in case she missed anything. The privateer was sailing west, fast. *Catch him*, she was thinking. *Catch him*. The whole of the *Narwhal* waited. Jack Strap was crouching by the helmsman. The helmsman was crouching by the wheel like a racing yachtsman. The captain was smiling, a cheery smile that did not fit his mad, stony eyes. *Narwhal* flung great fans of white spray back from her bows as she galloped across the low blue hills of water after the American ship. Kate watched the men on the American's stern: little black pin-dots of heads, tiny square shoulders, like the dolls she did not want to play with.

But they were not dolls. They were people. And as people will when you draw closer to them, they grew.

They grew until Kate could see the sun flashing off the brass buttons of their coats. They grew until she could see that the paint on the hull was not just stained and streaked, but chipped and shattered – by shot, Kate guessed.

"Point-blank," said the sailor who had loaded the gun to the sailor who had aimed the gun.

Kate said, "What does that mean?"

The aimer did not look at her; he was too busy, squinting across the sea at the privateer. He said, as if thinking about something else, "When you fire at long range, the ball drops. Point-blank is when you be so close unto she that the ball don't drop at all."

Ahead, something happened to the American's sails. They had been in line ahead, swelling tight as pigeon-breasts. Now they flattened, and the ship turned sideways-on to the *Narwhal*'s bow.

On the *Narwhal*'s poop deck, Jack Strap screamed something that sounded like a string of curses. Aloft, canvas roared and drummed in the breeze.

"She'll fight it out," said the sailor, sucking his teeth.

The *Narwhal* cruised slowly on down. Kate found her palms were sweating. "What now?" she said to the aimer.

The aimer did not answer. The loader said, "We'll rake her. Shoot 'er in the back end windows. In 'er weak spot, like. So the shot goes all the way down the deck inside. Dreadful mess, it'll make."

"Stop her chatter," said the gunner.

The *Narwhal* was heading for the privateer's stern. Kate held her breath, waiting for the first of the guns to line up. Just before they did, canvas rattled and roared on the American's foremast, and her nose came round. Instead of the chipped and faded gilt of the stern, Kate found she was looking at a long black-and-white side, a side with the gun ports triced up, lined with the eyes of cannon-muzzles.

"Wery prettily done," said the loader, licking lips that appeared suddenly to have gone dry. "Now we do be for it."

Jack Strap bellowed again.

The world exploded round Kate's ears.

For what seemed like a year, there was only bitter smoke, and humming splinters, and the salty planks of the deck against her face.

Afterwards, she worked out that the American must have fired first, the *Narwhal* some ten seconds later. But mostly it sounded as if every gun in the world was firing together. Stinging white smoke billowed into her eyes. Somewhere, someone was shouting without words.

She coughed, tasting more sulphur. There was more shouting. The stunning crash came again and again.

Kate swallowed to clear the swarm of bees droning in her ears. The guns had fallen quiet. For a moment, she could hear the slosh of the swell, the creak of the rigging. All she could see was a white fog of smoke.

There was a cool breeze on her face. The deck tilted under her feet. The white fog thinned. She took a breath. *Narwhal* was sailing again. For a second, she was relieved. Then the fog blew away completely, and the relief blew away too.

Out of the smoke came the black-and-white hull of the American, high as a low cliff. There was shouting from her deck, the thunder of flogging canvas.

Kate realized Keane was standing beside her. She remembered to be pleased that he was alive. But the thought did not last, because of the grim way he was watching the gold-encrusted stern windows of the privateer as it turned away. He said, "Mind yourself." Kate could not understand why.

"Stern chasers," said Keane.

Then she understood.

Fifty yards away, above the tall gilt windows of the aftercabin, two black eyes were staring straight at her. The eyes were poised one either side of a gilt nameboard that said THANKSGIVING in big, Roman letters appropriate for Mars, god of war. They were perfectly circular, those eyes. There was a flicker of something glowing behind them. Kate's tongue was sticking to the roof of her mouth.

The eyes were the muzzles of cannon.

There was a huge, stunning BANG. The muzzles disappeared in a house-sized bloom of smoke. Something whirred like a partridge past Kate's ear. There was a crash. A thread of fire touched her cheek. I'm hit, she thought.

There were groans and screams. High above, there was a mighty creaking. Kate put her hand to her cheek. It left a tiny dab of blood on her finger. Scratch, she thought.

Someone cried in a weird, howling voice, "The mainmast!"

The smoke had gone. The privateer was a hundred yards away now, and the gap of blue water between the ships was opening.

But Kate was not looking at the privateer. She was standing with her head back and her mouth open, watching the mainmast. The balls from the privateer's sternchasers had chewed a great half-moon out of the spar eight feet above the deck. Ropes were twanging and parting, coiling and swinging against the blue sky. Wearily, the mast was leaning to port, towards the water.

There were sailors on the mast. Low down, they were holding on. Higher up, the pendulum effect was making the movement sharper and harder.

Bryanston was on the royal yard. Kate could see his face, a little white blob up there. He was looking at her. Even at this range, she could feel his fury. *You were ordered up here*, he seemed to be saying. *Not me.* The mast leaned over as far as it could, far over the heaving Atlantic swell. Then the rigging brought it to a sharp stop.

Bryanston kept on going.

He went off that yard with his arms and legs spread, as if he were trying to teach himself to fly. But he did not fly. He went over twice, end over end, with a long despairing yell. Then he hit the sea feet-first, with a surprisingly small splash. Kate watched in a sort of paralysed horror. She thought she saw an arm wave.

But by that time, the mast had fallen in too, and pandemonium had broken loose.

She thought, *But for Jago, that would have been me.*

Jack Strap was bellowing from the quarterdeck. The sails on the other masts were full, and the ship was slewing sideways down the wind. The privateer had hove-to, and hung there watching the *Narwhal's* struggles. Kate yelled, "Help! Man overboard!" Nobody seemed to hear. Then she was knocked sprawling by a sailor with an axe, running towards the tangle of rope and timber that had once been the mainmast. She grabbed his arm and yelled again, "There's a boy overboard!"

The sailor looked at her blankly. He said, "There'll be more than boys in the water if we don't clear this away." He pulled his arm free.

The ship was rolling in the heavy swell. Keane bent over her where she lay in the lee of the bulwark. "You all right?" he said.

Kate nodded.

"I'll join ye," said Keane. "If I don't impose?"

"Not at all," said Kate. Keane sat down with a courtier's elegance.

Something hit the hull with a bang like a giant hammer.

"That'll be the mast," said Keane, philosophically.

"Old Pa Neptune'll be using it as a battering ram."

Kate had her eye to a bullet hole in the planking. There was no sign of Bryanston: only the huge blue sea. Please, she was thinking. Not drowned. The next thump knocked the wooden wall back into her nose.

"It's still attached, d'ye see?" said Keane, stifling an artificial yawn. "By a lot of shrouds and halyards and bits of string and the Lord knows what all. And the waves are banging it—"

Boom, went the mast against the side.

"Into the lower deck, by the sound of it," said Keane. "Hope it spoils some biscuit." He seemed quite unworried that it would sink the ship, too. "Absolutely *hate* weevily biscuit."

Kate said, "Bryanston was up the mast when it went."

They both peered through the bullet holes. "He could swim," said Keane. "But we're drifting."

The wind was dropping. The swell was becoming a long, glassy heave.

A long way away, up what wind there was, the privateer lay rolling. There was something else up there, too: a ship's boat, crawling across the water, its oars dipping like a beetle's legs.

The oars halted. Someone was bending over

the bow of the boat, fishing something out of the water. It was impossible to tell at this distance, but it could have been Bryanston. Kate hoped passionately that it was.

There were new shouts, the thwack of an axe. The mainmast drifted clear, a tangle of timber and cordage wallowing like a sea monster in the glassy swell.

It was getting dark, Kate realized.

"Now they'll have to jury rig. Put up a makeshift, y'know," said Keane. "That'll take 'em all night."

Kate said, "What if the Yankees come at us in the night?"

"We can still shoot," said Keane. "Besides, there's no wind. They'll wait till the morning, I expect. Something to look forward to. Have a biscuit?"

Kate realized she was hungry. She took the rock-hard biscuit. As she gnawed it, she thought about Jago. He was being kind to her, and had probably saved her life. But at the same time, he had signalled the privateer with the bottom of his tobacco box. He might easily be a spy. But apart from Keane, he was the only person on the *Narwhal* she trusted.

Her duty was to tell someone about him.

But she thought of Strap's raw-beef face, and the captain, remote on the quarterdeck. She thought of herself, in a mess under false pretences. And she knew that duty or no duty, she was not going to utter a word.

A wounded man was roaring from the cockpit, below the gun deck. Kate's stomach felt queasy, her skin cold and shivery. She decided that she was not looking forward to the morning at all.

10

Hangman's Knot

She spent that night under the bulwark, close to Keane, sleeping the sleep of the utterly exhausted. The cat came and slept on top of her. Jago was up the mast. The flames in the riggers' lanterns burned like orange spearheads in the still air as they worked. There was no sign of the privateer, but it would still be out there in the dark, waiting.

At two bells of the morning watch – five a.m. on land – Kate woke from a fitful sleep into a cold, grey twilight world. The riggers had done their work. Onto the stump of the mainmast had been grafted another spar. In the half-darkness it looked awkward and dwarfish. But it was unquestionably a spar. It filled Kate's chest with bubbles of hope. She sat up, stuck her head under the pump.

The sun was climbing above the eastern horizon,

making a red-hot path in the grey metal of the sea. Keane had been asleep beside her. He stirred and looked overboard. "Oogh," he said. "Straight up and down. Paddy's hurricane."

"What?" said Kate.

"The wind," said Keane. He stretched his thin arms, yawned, turned through a full circle. Three-quarters of the way round, he stopped, became rigid. "Oh," he said. "Oh, lawks-a-mussy."

Kate followed his eyes.

The sea was not entirely smooth. Here and there, fields of ripples marred its glassy surface, like the marks of a giant breath on a huge windowpane. In the middle of one of those patches, perhaps five miles away, the piled-up sails of a big schooner leaned pink in the dawning sun. Kate recognized the ship, because she had spent the whole of the previous day staring at it. The American.

"Back they come," said Keane. "To finish the job." For the first time since Kate had known him, there was no laugh in his voice. She felt a chill that had nothing to do with the red, heatless sun.

The privateer came on.

The deck shook as if someone were rolling iron skittle-balls down a wooden alley. *Narwhal* was running out her guns.

"They'll have the legs of us today," said Keane. "Off we go again."

The laugh was back in his voice, but Kate could not be amused. *Narwhal's* new, stubby mast meant she could move again, but slowly and clumsily. And the American had already shown that she was quick in the water.

Aft, Jack Strap was shouting hoarsely at a group of seamen with cutlasses. He sounded tired and angry. There was a padding of horny soles on deck, and Jago crouched down beside Kate. "Pretty mornin'," he said, screwing up his blue eyes at the sun. He must have been working all night, Kate thought, up in the rigging. But he did not show any signs. He yawned and stretched his arms. His shirt fell down his arms to the knotty muscles of his shoulders. On the left shoulder was a tattoo she had not seen before. There was a sheaf of pikes and cannon and lightning bolts. On a shield in the middle, written in Roman letters appropriate to Mars, god of war, was the word THANKSGIVING.

It was the same name and the same script that had appeared on the gilt nameboard on the stern of the American privateer.

Kate stared at him with her mouth open. He winked at her. He said, "There's not much in a name. You keep mum, now."

Kate closed her mouth. She nodded. She was sure he was a spy. But it was even clearer this morning. Better a kind spy than Sprat or the captain.

Keane said, "She's heaving to."

Across the water, the privateer had hauled her topsails aback. Something was happening under her port side. "What're they doing?" said Jago.

"Lowering a boat," said Kate.

The boat crept across the water towards them. The sun was well up now, a burning yellow eye that spread a glow in Kate's blood. The Americans were coming to talk, not attack. Nobody was going to get hurt.

The boat grew under the sun, oar blades shining at each dip. There were eight men rowing, a man in a blue coat steering in the stern, a white flag flapping on a staff at his shoulder.

"Stagger me endways!" said Keane. "It's Bryanston!"

Bryanston was standing rigidly to attention. *He's not drowned*, thought Kate. *Thank goodness he's not drowned.* As the boat came closer she saw that his face was shut tight, the lower lip jutting, the brow scowling.

"Looks upset about something," said Keane.

The man in the stern of the longboat spoke a few

words. It was a casual remark, not the mastiff-like bark in which Jack Strap liked to give his orders. The rowers stopped rowing, leaned on their oars. They sat there, rising and falling on the long swell, relaxed as haymakers at mowing's end, under the ugly snouts of *Narwhal's* four starboard-side guns.

"Howdy!" cried the man in the rowing boat's stern. "I guess you dropped something."

Bryanston stood stock still, scowling. Kate felt very sorry for him.

The captain of the *Narwhal* walked to the quarterdeck rail. He was smiling kindly, as if American privateers' boats brought back members of his crew every day of the week. He said, "Much obliged to you. Come no closer just now, if you please." Kate thought the eyes above the smile had a mad, stony look.

The American said, "We came to tell you this here young gentleman is alive. Do you want him back?"

The captain said, soft as a cat's purr, "You are surpassing kind."

The American laughed. "Real pretty," he said. "We don't got no use for him. So I guess you can feed him until we take your ship."

The captain's smile did not waver. He said, "Sir, you will not take my ship."

The American said, "No sense in argufying 'bout that. Time will tell, Captain. Now I purpose to come alongside of you here to let this boy aboard, if you have no objection."

"None whatsoever," said the captain. "I thank you extremely."

The American bowed, and said, "I'll thank ye to observe the flag of truce till we're out of shot, sir."

The captain bowed back. "Happy to oblige, sir," he said.

The captain murmured something to Jack Sprat. Jack Sprat bellowed, "Run in the guns, gunners, lively!" *Narwhal's* timbers shook to the rumble of the gun-carriages. The ports slammed shut. "At your SERVICE!" bellowed Sprat.

The boat came alongside. Bryanston climbed up the steps and through the entry port.

The American said in a quiet voice, "Row her home, boys." Jack Sprat looked as if blood might squirt out of his ears. The boat crawled away over the sea.

The captain spoke quietly to Strap. Strap did some more bellowing. Canvas appeared at *Narwhal's* yards. The helmsman wound the wheel over, and the ship's nose turned east, back towards England, two hundred miles over the horizon. Slowly, thought Kate, dry-mouthed. Far too slowly, with her stubby new mast.

She felt eyes on her. She turned and looked at the quarterdeck. Bryanston was standing beside the captain. They were both watching her. Bryanston was looking smug. The captain had lost his smile. His face was heavy and angry, and the skin around his lips looked whitish.

Jago gripped her arm. The captain's finger came out and pointed at the pair of them. "You!" he barked. "Here!"

They walked aft. Kate felt as she felt at school when she had not learned her lesson because she had been watching the caulkers in the dry dock and she was called forward for the strap.

"Up here!" said the captain. He had recovered control of his voice.

Kate and Jago walked up. Jago hissed, "Don't say nothing, nohow. Irregardless. You'll be all right, I promise ye." The marine at the bottom of the steps stood aside.

Kate told herself, *You have at last got to the captain, which is what you have been trying to do ever since you came aboard. Now is your chance.*

But the captain's eyes were about as friendly as the guns of the *Thanksgiving*, five miles astern and gaining.

The captain pointed to a spot in front of him. "Stand there," he said. "Now, Mr Bryanston. Tell this young man what you told me."

Bryanston's clothes looked wrinkled and shrunk. He said, "I was picked up by the dam' Yankees, sir, begging your pardon. They treated me well, sir. I heard a conversation between their captain and their … first lieutenant that gave me to believe that there was one of their own aboard the *Narwhal*."

"One of their own aboard the *Narwhal*," said the captain. He was smiling now, the same tense smile he had used when he had parleyed with the captain of the *Thanksgiving*.

Kate thought of the THANKSGIVING tattoo on Jago's arm. She kept her eyes front. She wanted to speak but her throat had seized up.

"And that this person," said the captain, "had conveyed to agents of this rascally damned Yankee privateer a notion of the planned cruise of His Britannic Majesty King George's ship *Narwhal* the way this damned privateer could fall upon her and make a prize of her. And that this person had come aboard in Pembroke Dock, masquerading as another."

Kate tried to say something. Jago had joined in Pembroke Dock, it was true. He had signalled from the royal yard. He had the THANKSGIVING tattoo. But he had been her friend.

The captain said, "You are not Master Edward Fortescue, sir. Sirrah, you are a spy in our midst."

Kate felt the blood drain out of her head, the cool breeze playing in her open mouth. He was looking at her and nobody else. She said, "No—"

"You stand condemned out of the mouths of your friends," said the captain. "I have no idea of and no interest in the means you used to communicate with them. I know we may all die tomorrow. But I know that the penalty for spying is death, and that you will pay the penalty before we each pay ours."

"Wait— " said Kate.

"There is no time," said the captain. "At dawn tomorrow, you will expiate your crimes. Marines, take this person from here and clap him in irons." He swung his head at Jago. "And, schoolmaster, you will fashion for your charge a hempen collar, all complete."

Jago grinned. He actually grinned all over his face. He said, "Aye, aye, sir."

Hard hands grabbed Kate, one under each arm. She wanted to explain. But she was crying now, and a great salty lump in her throat was getting in the way of the words.

The hands dragged her away. They pitched her into a black, evil-smelling cabin no bigger than a cupboard. They ordered a dirty seaman called Jasper Bones to sit outside the door. They slammed the door, and shot the bolts.

There was darkness.

11

Deadman's Bend

Kate sat for a long time staring into the darkness. It was so intense that red shapes floated in front of her eyeballs. After a while, she had no way of telling how long, the numbness wore off, and she began to think.

The thought in the front of her mind was that the captain had meant what he said, and that tomorrow at dawn they were going to hang her from the yardarm.

She must have slept. She woke in the dark, still thinking about hanging. It took her something like half an hour to peel that thought back, like a curtain. What lay behind the curtain was better. It was that she was a girl, and she had come on board by accident, as a result of a succession of accidents, some of them caused by Damn Yankee, the cat that someone had sent her. She could prove that she was a girl. That would save her life. But she would have to go back to Megan. And Megan would carry out her plan of moving to Cardiff, and Kate would land up in the scullery, half underground, scouring pots with bunches of chain and caustic soda. It would be a hideous sort of life.

But at least it would not end at dawn.

Kate found that the tears were slithering down her face. She felt as if she were going mad. Other children had mothers and fathers who stopped things like this happening to them. Kate had only herself.

She had had only herself since her mother had left. She had learned that if you wanted things to happen, you had to make them happen. In this case, she had to attract attention.

She began to shout.

It is not difficult to shout when you are due to be hanged in a few hours' time. She roared and yelled until the darkness was full of noise. When she stopped, her ears were ringing.

But apart from the stretch and groan of the ship's timbers, there was no other sound.

That was not quite true.

There was a scratching, the sort of scratching a mouse might have made if it was wearing gloves. It was coming from the direction of the door.

She said, quietly now, "Who's there?"

A muffled voice said, "Keane. I'm coming in. Only shut up, would you?"

Suddenly Kate was hot with excitement and relief. The door opened. Yellow light flooded in. It was so bright it dazzled her. When her eyes had accustomed themselves to the glare, she saw that it came from a horn lantern with a single candle burning in it. The light picked out the flattish bones of Keane's face, the Norman arches of his humorous eyebrows. There was a smell of drink.

She said, "How did you get in?"

He said. "Stole old Bones a quart of rum. The whole ship knows we're to be blowed out of the water when the Yankee catches us. Bones is an old soak, particularly when he's scared. So come on."

"Come on?" Kate did not understand.

"Out of here," said Keane.

"But where?" said Kate.

"On deck, I imagine," said Keane. "Hide."

"But what then?" said Kate.

"Listen," said Keane. "In not so long, they are going to drop a noose round your neck, and haul you up to the yardarm. And soon after that, at the present rate, a damned big American privateer is going to mince us up. There's a moon. I've been watching. Jago says he's gaining."

Kate said, "Jago's the spy. Not me."

Keane said, "It was Jago sent me to get you out. Now you come on." His face was shining with sweat in the yellow lantern light. He turned away. Kate followed him, stepped over the snoring figure of Jasper Bones in the doorway. Kate shot the bolt again. She felt that she might be dreaming.

Except that she knew this was real.

They passed along what seemed like a maze of passages. They were on the lower deck, Kate guessed, below the gun deck. It seemed to be night. The lantern light gleamed on slung hammocks, holding their sleepers like moth pupae in a disused shed. Except that this place was far from disused. Even with half the ship asleep, there was still the feeling that came from Uncle Owen's shop when the door was locked.

Except that this time, it was not like waiting outside the room. This time, it was like being the patient in the chair.

"On deck," said Keane. "There are no lights."

They came to the foot of the companionway. Kate found she was swallowing continuously, but her mouth was dry.

She was thinking, *Perhaps I should have stayed*

put. Explained. Running away will make it worse.

As she put her foot on the first step, voices sounded above. Big voices. Officers' voices.

"Down," said Keane.

She ran after him, quiet as she could, following the jump and flick of the lantern. The footsteps above were slower. The voices were talking about pumps. The main pumps were amidships, on the lower deck. The knock and thump of the seesaw handles came through the boards underfoot.

Keane kept going down. The air became sour and ugly in Kate's nostrils. Suddenly there was gravel underfoot. They were on the ballast, as far down as you could go.

Last time, it had been Bryanston that had led her down here. This time, the ballast was different. The gravel felt wet and spongy, as if it was saturated with water. Kate thought, *The ship is sinking. We will get trapped here.* She thought of what Bryanston had told her. There were bodies buried in this ballast. It was all a mistake. She would have liked to be back in her little wooden cell, in the safe dark. But she felt paralysed, able to think but unable to speak or act.

The lantern made a little yellow sphere in the black dark. Threads of water gleamed in the ballast, coming and going with the roll of the ship.

Out there in the inky black, a small voice said, "Braow?"

"S'welp me," said Keane, in a voice not altogether steady. "It's Dam' Yankee."

The cat trotted into the yellow light, ran up Kate's right-hand side, and arranged itself across her shoulders like a fur collar. She had almost forgotten that warm, soft things existed.

Keane led the way through the maze of boxes and barrels. They squeezed into a little room among the cases. There were a couple of cushions, and a meat bone, covered with the tiny chisel marks of rats' teeth. "Nobody can get through," he said. "We come down here when we've prigged some prog from Cookie. Here." He gave her a biscuit and a lump of cheese.

Kate gnawed at it, and felt better.

Kate said, "And what now?"

He shrugged, looked at the wet gravel floor. "Jago said ..."

"Said what?"

"Said go to the Americans. Are you really a spy?"

Kate said, "Of course I'm not. Why did Bryanston say I was?"

Keane shrugged. He said, "Dunno. Funny thing, though. He wasn't lying. He thought he was telling the truth."

Kate said, "What—"

"No, honestly," said Keane. "Bryanston's a swine. But he's not enough of a swine to tell a story that will get you ..." He dropped his eyes.

"Hanged," said Kate. It all seemed a long way away, as if it was happening to someone else. But there was the dim sense that the walls of the locked room in her mind were bulging, and hints of riot and mayhem were beginning to spill out of the cracks. "So what, then?"

Keane said, "He told me someone on that American was saying that a person had come aboard the *Narwhal* in Pembroke. The American said something to the effect that they had landed this person down the coast, in the night, and sent them to join up with *Narwhal*. Before they joined, they'd found out what our orders were. And they'd got a signal. There was one other thing. 'The child's still aboard,' they said. Still talking about the spy." Keane shrugged his shoulders, and looked miserable. "You see?" he said.

Kate felt dizzy, but strong in the mind. Jago, she thought. It all fitted Jago. But Bryanston had said his say in front of the captain. And now he had said it, he would never have the courage to unsay it. She said, "And if you believe I'm a spy, why did you let me out?"

Keane cranked his eyes up on to hers. "I don't think I do believe it," he said. "Besides." He fell quiet. There was only the knock of the pumps.

"What?" said Kate.

Keane said, "My mama's dead. My papa's dead. I'm a follower with no one to follow. I've nothing ashore, and no prospects at sea. I thought you were a friend. If you're not a spy, then I hate the people who will hurt you after they've false-accused you. If you are a spy, then spies can't be so bad after all. It's a bit of a muddle, really."

Kate knew that if there was anyone she could confess to, it was Keane. She took a deep breath. She said, "I'm not Henry Fortescue. And I'm a girl, not a boy."

Keane opened his mouth to say something. No sound came out. His skin had turned pale and waxy. He said, "Not possible."

Kate felt the hot prickle of tears. Nobody believed her. Not even Keane. She said, "It's true. Really."

For some seconds, Keane made a noise like an owl gargling. Then he shut his mouth with a snap. "Sorry," he said. "How?"

Kate told him.

When she had finished, he turned a colour that was hard to distinguish in the lamplight, but was probably red. He said, "Blow me, Harry, er, Mistress Kate, er … well, blow me down."

Kate had begun to see things clearly. She said, "So it's not me that's the spy. It's Jago."

He had just got his mouth shut. It fell open again. She explained about the snuffbox, and the tattoo. "So I'd be grateful if you could go to the captain, and explain," she said. "He'll listen to you, no doubt."

There was a sinking feeling in her stomach. She thought of Megan, and the scullery. For ever, in Cardiff.

Keane was looking unhappy. He said, "I'm not so sure."

"What do you mean?"

Keane said, "The captain. He … he's never wrong, if you see what I mean. At least he's never been known to admit it."

"Even if a boy turns into a girl?"

Keane nodded hard, his eyes circular in the lamplight. He seemed a lot more eager to please since Kate had told him the truth. "Of course, that's different. But … well, look." He pointed at the ground.

Kate had for some time been aware that their feet were wet, but when you think you can see a way to save yourself from death by hanging, you can be wet up to your neck and hardly notice a thing. The reason her feet were wet was that the water was three inches over the gravel now. The pumps were clunking away like the beating of a wooden heart.

"He's got a few things on his mind," said Keane. "He won't listen."

Kate had already taken the first step. The second was easier. "I'll take my clothes off," she said. "I'll parade like Venus on the deck. There are ... differences."

Keane giggled weirdly. He was definitely scarlet with embarrassment. He said, "He wouldn't notice if Mrs Siddons herself wagged her arse on the quarterdeck, er, begging your pardon, Mistress Kate. But what there was, was Jago had a message. His message was this: 'Get 'im out, and hide while ye may, my anzums.'" He put on a grim masquerade of Jago's accent. "'And when they catches us, go to Ameriky.'"

"Ameriky?" said Kate.

"That's what he said. But he's a spy."

Kate thought of Jago. She thought of him as a spy, coming aboard with a cat in a basket, which had landed up on her doorstep. Now it looked as if he was at least as responsible as Keane for letting her out of prison. She was sure he was a spy.

But he was a very strange kind of spy. A kind of spy, she felt, more trustworthy than the officers of His Britannic Majesty's sloop-of-war *Narwhal*.

The roll of the ship became a pitch, as if it was changing direction on the waves. Somewhere behind them, there was a heavy crash. Keane said, "That was a cannon-ball." Then *Narwhal's* own guns spoke their ear-numbing thunder. The pumps kept on.

And there was another sound. Out beyond the boxes that walled the little room where they sat, there was the squelch of feet in wet gravel. A lot of feet. Keane quickly shuttered the lantern. The hold was dark again.

But not completely dark. Through the doorway by which they had entered there came a faint yellow flicker. The sweat turned cold on Kate's body.

Someone grabbed a cask, rolled it away. Another one went. Yellow light poured in, making her screw up her eyes. The cat jumped down and scooted into the dark. There were men with lanterns, stooping under the low wooden roof.

"Mr Fortescue," said the harsh voice of Lieutenant John Walters, alias Jack Strap. "Your friends are arriving, it seems. But I fear you will not see them, because it wants only fifteen minutes till dawn."

Kate said, "No—"

"Gag him," said Strap.

Someone thrust a rag into Kate's mouth, and bound it tight. Someone else pinioned her arms. Someone knocked Keane flat on his face. He looked small, his arms thin as sticks as they picked him up and dragged him out of the yellow light and into the darkness of the hold. She struggled, trying to run after Keane. But they were men, and she was an eleven-year-old girl. She tried to yell, to tell them it was a terrible mistake. But the gag filled her mouth, salty with her tears now. The hands gripped her painfully under the arms and she was hauled away herself, upwards, towards the grey light that was already seeping down the companionway from the deck.

It was nearly dawn.

12

Shroud Knot

It was very nearly dawn. Kate's knees seemed to be made of water. The *Narwhal* was wallowing across a low swell frosted with wind, leaning over to starboard, sails full. Beyond the ship's side, the sea was covered with silver streaks. Kate glanced astern.

The American ship was perhaps a quarter of a mile away, wearing a white moustache of spray under the long beak of her bowsprit.

"Your friends can't help you now," said the harsh voice of Lieutenant Walters. "The noose."

A figure stepped forward out of the half-darkness. There were other figures there, lined up, watching. She saw Bryanston and the poor little Beans looking pale and confused. "Not quite ready yet, zur, my anzum."

It was Jago. Lieutenant Walters sputtered like a

fuse, getting ready to explode. Kate was thinking that the gag tasted disgusting, and that she must tell somebody, and that she was more frightened that she had ever been, and that she hated Jago, because it was he who had got her into all this trouble.

Then, with the eye furthest from Lieutenant Walters, Jago winked.

It was a big wink. And for some reason, despite the loathing she felt for him, it made Kate feel much better.

Lieutenant Walters barked, "Explain this to your pupils, schoolmaster."

"Deed I will, zur," said Jago. Kate suddenly realized that his accent sounded overdone, as if he was putting it on. He walked over to the mainmast. When he came back he had a rope's end in his hand. The other end of the rope went up, up into the dark pre-dawn sky. Kate followed it with her eyes. It went to the yardarm, the outside end of the mainyard. In ten minutes, she would be up at the yardarm herself. Her knees gave. Oh, no, she thought. Please.

But she could not speak.

She felt arms holding her up. She saw Jago's face again. He was grinning and nodding. His mouth was close to her ear. He said, "It's not what 'ee thinks."

Someone was making a noise. She recognized the voice, high and piercing. It was Keane. He was shouting. "You can't do this! It's not fair. He's not Fortescue! He's a girl!"

Jack Sprat's voice said, "Tie him up. We'll flog him after."

"No!" yelled Keane. "She—"

His voice was cut off sharply. A sailor carried him away, legs kicking. Bryanston watched him, face pale and stiff. He was terrified, Kate realized. Too terrified to speak out even against someone being hanged unjustly. Her heart was knocking like the hooves of a galloping horse.

"Tell 'ee what," said Jago, reasonable as if he was teaching bowlines in the Rope School. "Let's give this year kit an' caboodle a try. This year rope goes up, see, all the way to the yardarm. Then it travels through a block, a pulley, like, back to another pulley by the mast, and down again to where these 'ere five good men stands a-waitin' to run away forrard, the way they will hoist this year accused unfortnit up aloft. So I'll just hitch the end of him to this 'ere rail, and these men'll run away forrard. For rehearsal, like, *hif* you takes me meaning."

Jack Strap said, "Come along, schoolmaster. Look lively."

"Heasy, Jacky boy," said Jago with a winning smile. "Right first time, that's the ticket, eh?"

Jack Strap's face turned the colour of raw beef. He said, "Why, you damned insolent—"

"Run, boys," said Jago.

The five sailors spat on their hands. Kate shut her eyes. Their feet thundered on the deck. There was a strange and horrible *thunk*. Jack Strap started screaming oaths.

Kate opened her eyes.

The men were down the other end of the deck, holding the rope, which was loose in their hands. They were looking upwards. Their mouths were hanging open. Jack Strap was looking upwards, too. His mouth was open, ready to bellow. His eyes were bulging from his head so that the whites showed all the way round the pupils. Kate thought, *What is happening?*

Jago was the only one not looking upwards. He was looking at Kate, grinning. "Fixed that properjob, dinwe?" he said, in a voice that sounded surprisingly loud above the sudden blanket of quiet that had fallen over *Narwhal's* deck.

Then there was a creaking and a twanging of ropes. And for the second time in thirty-six hours, *Narwhal's* mainmast fell down.

That was the end of the silence.

Kate felt Jago tuck her under his arm, and run. Her eyes were blurred, and she would not have known her own name if you had asked her. But she could hear a roaring and a yelling, and see above the poop the triple tower of the American's yellowish-cream sails, and the jut of her long bowsprit over *Narwhal's* poop rail. Then once again there was the huge thunder of the explosion, and the world vanished in a chord of flying metal and a pall of white smoke.

Someone was doing something to her gag and the ropes that bound her arms. They fell away. Somewhere there was the rattle of musket shot, higher and sharper than cannons. The smoke cleared.

There was no mainmast any more. But on the windward side of the boat, there was something new – a long wall of black-and-white checks with masts rising beyond it. The *Thanksgiving* was alongside.

A rope snaked over the American's bulwark. Something on the end clattered on the deck. It looked like a miniature anchor. A grapnel. It caught in the tangled cordage that had once been the mainshrouds.

Jago put his mouth to her ear. His eyes were shifting to and fro. He looked worried. He said,

"Sorry about that, my anzum. Little trick with the 'anging cord. Pulled the lanyards out of the mainshroud deadeyes. Long and short of it is, there's nothing to keep the mast up any more. So it come down, 'stead o' Kate going up."

Kate's mouth dried out. "Kate?" she croaked.

Jago grinned. "That's you, en 'er? Jago knowed. So now if you don't mind, you'd better come along o' me onto the old *Thanksgiving*."

She said, "Why?"

He was not smiling. "Because if you stays 'ere, and *Narwhal* don't sink, Jack Strap'll see you 'ung, sharpish. In addition to which, you are expected. Now you come arter me."

Kate was dizzy. She knew there was something else. It arrived in her mind. She said, "Keane."

"Ah yes," said Jago. "We'll find 'im. Now you run along, there."

"Where?"

He pointed to the blank side of the American ship. "There," he said.

There was a crash of guns. *Narwhal* shudered. More white smoke erupted from between the two ships. *No*, thought Kate. *The knees won't work. I can't move.*

And they wouldn't. And she couldn't.

The smoke eddied. By her feet, a small voice said,

"Brraoow?"

It was Damn Yankee.

She bent to pick him up. He skipped out of the way, looked back at her, tail up. It was the same look he had given her on the quay at Pembroke when the coachman and the crowd had been hunting her. Tail waving like a flag, he trotted off into the smoke.

Kate's knees stiffened She went after him.

Men were running. They had cutlasses in their hands. They were yelling. None of them paid any attention to Kate as she followed the cat forward, across the wreckage of the mainmast and its rigging.

Damn Yankee arrived at the steps that led up onto the platform of the fo'c'sle. There was a knot of men up there, struggling to lever round the carriage of a huge gun so they could aim it at the American. *Narwhal's* deck was on the same level as *Thanksgiving's*. There was a twelve-foot gap of grey water sloshing between the ships. The gap shrank, growing narrower. Three heads came up from behind the American's bulwark. Their owners paid no attention to Kate. They jumped across the four-foot gap and went for the men with the gun, waving cutlasses. There was the evil hiss and clash of steel on steel.

"Go on," said a voice. It was Keane. "America's a step away."

Damn Yankee said, "Braow," and jumped across the gap. Kate thought: *He has gone over to the enemy.*

But she had followed him before. And there was no reason not to follow him now. She went after him. The sides of the ships ground together. She half-saw Keane land. There was a lot of noise, the yells of men, more steel on more steel. The air was full of things that hummed and whined. Bullets, thought somebody who must have been Kate, though she seemed a long way away.

Keane was crouching beside her, grinning. They were on pale, scrubbed planks. American planks. In the foggy depths of Kate's mind, a brass band seemed to be playing, in time to someone shooting muskets up in the rigging. Oh, dear, thought Kate. I do feel faint. Keane's pale face with the hymn-book-pause eyebrows zoomed away down a long tunnel.

Into darkness.

13

True Lover's Knot

There was noise, a rumbling and a clattering in the darkness. The noise was extremely alarming, particularly because the darkness was extremely dark, worse even than the inky black of the condemned cell on *Narwhal.*

Then Kate realized that it would be lighter if she opened her eyes. So she did.

She was lying in the lee of a low deckhouse. The air was full of cannon-smoke. Above her a mainmast soared into the blue sky – a mainmast with blackened and peeling varnish but with its rigging intact, and a huge fore-and-aft sail sweeping up to a gaff.

In the foreground, there was a face.

It was the face of a man. The eyes were blue. The hair, which fell almost to the shoulders of the coat, was dark red. It was a thin face, pale and tired-looking. It looked as if the mind behind it did a lot of thinking. It was a familiar face, the way that a face you half-glimpse every time you comb your hair is familiar.

As Kate watched, the face turned bright red. And in the second it took the blood to rise, her heart pounded once, hard, and seemed to stop.

The man said, "Kate. Alive and well, by the powers!"

She opened her mouth to speak. Her mind was swirling with pictures from a time when she had been too little to think properly, or notice things right. She tried to speak, but her throat was full of sand.

There were arms around her. Her face was against a rough serge coat that smelt of sweat and gunpowder. The man said, "So we found you." There was something in his voice that might have been tears.

Kate had another go at her voice. There was a question she needed to ask, but it was such an important one she scarcely dared ask it. She said, "Are you my father?"

He looked at her. "Are you Kate Griffiths, sometime ward of Owen Griffiths, the barber of Pembroke?"

Kate tried to say, "Yes." It came out as a squeak.

His face was solemn. "Then it looks very much as if I am. Kate, my dear, I and your mother are the happiest people alive."

The brass band between Kate's ears started up again. No, thought Kate. I am the happiest person alive.

Somewhere behind the deckhouse, a man's voice yelled. Her father straightened up. "If you will excuse me … a few more minutes, after all these years?" He got up and strode aft.

Keane was beside her. He looked pale and nervous. He summoned up a grin. "Well," he said. "You seem to be … among friends."

Even with her head spinning, Kate could recognize his loneliness. She said, "We are."

He smiled at her. She sat up. She felt at the same time deliriously happy and very ill.

The rumbling had ceased. It had been the sound of guns run in, and the clatter of gun ports closing. She stood up, supporting herself on the deckhouse. Half a mile of blue water away, something long and dark lay in the sea. It could have been a whale, but it was not a whale. Indistinct shapes wallowed about it in the water like the limbs of a kraken.

"All in the boats," said Keane. "Every man Jack of 'em. I counted 'em." He handed her a telescope.

She focused with difficulty. Into the disc of her vision swam three boats. There were perhaps thirty men in each, the captain at the helm of one, glaring eastward with his faint smile. In another stood Jack Strap, his face purple, bellowing something Kate was too far away to hear.

"They've got food," said Keane. "They've got water. They can be in Ireland in a day. The … skipper told me."

Kate kept the glass on the boats. She was searching the heads. She felt a million miles away, like a traveller in time surveying a different life. There was Bryanston and the Beans. There were a couple of sailors she recognized, and the cook. But there was a head missing. Her heart felt cold in her body. "Where's Jago?" she said.

"Year," said a voice, high above.

She looked up.

There was a spar sixty feet above her, sixty feet of curved yellow-cream canvas. There was someone standing on the spar, right at the peak where the huge Stars and Stripes billowed red, white and blue in the wind from the west. From below, it was hard to see who it was.

The figure jumped.

It slid down the curve of the sail like a child on a mudslide. For the last fifteen feet, it stood on its feet, digging in its heels to slow down until it arrived on the boom. And there it stood, lightly balanced against the roll of the ship, with the cat Damn Yankee in its arms.

Jago.

He jumped down. He was frowning. His eyes were blue and glittering, staring straight into Kate's. He said, "It weren't meant to get that far."

Kate said, "What?"

He said, "I dangered your life. I kept from you the truth. But I had to be sure who you was, see."

Kate said, "Sure?"

Jago was flushed a dull red under his mahogany tan. He said, "You come aboard with that cat Damn Yankee, that I left for you. And you was dressed like a lad, and you climbed to the maintruck, and you ate salt pork and biscuit, and I thought, Boil me in tar if that's a girl." He scowled and grinned at the same time. Kate wondered if his face would break in half. "But you was. You was axing me about this year cat, and I seed your father in your face but by then we'd met up with the *Thanksgiving*, and it was too dam' late to pipe up that you was who you was, case we all got 'ung. And when that cully Bryanston got 'is ideas mixed up and said you was the spy, I couldn't speak. Because if I'd spoken, I'd a been 'ung, and

Narwhal would 'ave got away, and you on board. And you'd have landed back in Pembroke, there. So that's about the long and the short of it. And year we are." He shut his mouth so tight his lips disappeared. He shook his head vigorously, so his pigtail lashed like a serpent between his shoulder blades. He took her by the arm, and pulled her aft. It was a new, odd Jago. For comfort, she grabbed Keane.

They walked aft, past sailors clearing up splintered wood and splicing cut lines. Someone had tipped a bucket of sawdust on a big puddle of what looked like blood. These people should be the enemy, thought Kate.

But they looked up from their work, and nodded, and winked. One of them said, "Jago. Bin on vacation?"

Jago, tight-lipped, pointed at Kate and Keane. The man said, "Oh," as if something long unexplained had suddenly become clear. Jago said, "Follow me."

They walked down a companionway into darkness. Jago shoved a door open. "Gwan," he said.

Kate walked in, still holding Keane by the arm. And suddenly, nothing was like anything had been before, or was ever going to be again.

Light was pouring in at the tall windows of the stern-cabin. There was a big hole where a cannon-shot had come through.

"Siddown," said Jago. "Miss."

Kate's knees were on the point of giving out. The tall man – her father – came out of another cabin. "All done," he said. "Now, then. Who's this?"

He was looking at Keane. Keane was looking at him. *He exists*, thought Kate. *My father exists, because Keane can see him, and he is the captain of this privateer.* Her knees went. She sat down so suddenly that she missed the chair.

Her father picked her up gently. "Kate," he said, as if it were a magic word. Then he said, "Food?"

Kate looked at Keane. Keane nodded. She nodded. Her father brought biscuits and something that might have been wine.

He said, "I'd better explain."

Very carefully, so as not to wake herself up, she nodded.

"We lost you," he said. "Your mother and I. Your Aunt Megan wrote letters, told us you were well, that you were the light of her eye."

Liar, Megan, thought Kate.

"Then she told us … you were dead."

Kate's mouth opened. *Megan*, she thought. How *could* you?

"A friend came out to Baltimore," said her father. "Before the war started. He took ship in Pembroke Dock, so of course he went to enquire about you at the barber's. And they told him you were dead, but the lady at the bakery –"

Mrs Jones the bakery, thought Kate. Dear Mrs Jones.

"– said there was a red-haired girl at the surgeon's. But my friend's ship was leaving, so there was no time to check. So when he told me, I just wondered. So when we set off on this cruise, me and my ship— "

"Your ship?"

"*Thanksgiving*," he said. "Ah. I should have explained. I'm in the sea trade. Cargo, in time of peace. Letters of marque, in time of war. It's a good trade."

Her father in the sea trade. Glory alleluia, thought Kate.

"Anyway," he said, "I dropped Jago ashore in the black of night at St Bride's Bay, up the coast from Pembroke. With Cougar."

"Cougar?"

"Cat. He's a Maine Coon. Special kind of American cat. Present for you, if Jago found you."

She said, "Dam' Yankee."

He frowned. Oh, no, thought Kate. He thinks

I'm talking to him. "That cat," she said. "That's what we called the cat."

He grinned. Then he roared with laughter. It was a huge noise, warm as a roomful of sunshine. He grabbed her in his arms, and hugged her. She hugged him back. Suddenly she was crying, the tears breaking from her like a wave. And she would not let go.

A good while later – it could have been ten minutes or ten days – they were eating more biscuits, Keane and Jago, and Kate and her father. And her father was managing at long last to explain.

"We left Jago to find you," he said. "Him and Cougar. We were to come back in five weeks, to pick him up, and you, if you … existed. But he lost all the money I gave him gambling. So he had to work to eat and the only trade he knew was the sea trade, so he signed up with King George's Navy, for the sake of the food." He grinned. "Only one who ever did it for that reason." Kate loved his grin. She loved all of him. He was her father, and he had brought a ship and fifty men to find her.

"So he made enquiries. But he found that *Narwhal* was going to sail that day. So he left a note for you round the cat's neck, telling you to come down to the ship and meet him, so he could take you away to St Bride's Bay, where we would be in a week to pick you up."

Kate said, "And Dam' ... Cougar ... shredded the note. I followed him on to *Narwhal*."

"And then Jago— "

"Dint know was she a boy or a girl, nohow," said Jago. "There she were on that ship. I dint mean to go to sea in she nohow. But with her on board, I couldn't see no ways out of it. I kept my eyes on 'er, though. I dint know, for sure, at first. Thought she might be a certain Fortescue."

"Tied the cat to the boot scraper," said Kate's father. "Jago, I despair of you."

Kate stood up. She said, "Are we going to America?"

"Baltimore," said her father. "That's where your mother is. That's where you live."

"So Keane's coming too."

"If he doesn't mind."

Kate looked at Keane. "Do you mind?" she said.

"Mistress Griffiths," said Keane. "I am very much obliged to you."

"Good," said her father.

Kate took a deep breath and tried to realize she was entering a new life, with a father who owned a ship and a mother who was waiting for her in the new world. She knew she was dreaming.

"Now then," said her father. "Your mother packed you some clothes, just in case."

"Girl's clothes?" said Kate.

"Of course," said her father.

Kate decided to test this dream once and for all. "The thing is," she said, "that a skirt does flutter so when you're making sail. Besides, she doesn't know my size."

Her father gazed upon her. He laughed. "Nor does she," he said. And he hugged her.

Over his arm, she saw Keane, watching them. She winked at him.

Jago said, "Arright, you idle lubbers. Back to school tomorrow."

Beyond the tall windows of the after cabin, *Narwhal*'s boats had hoisted their lugsails and were ploughing sullenly northeast, for the coast of Ireland. The Yankee privateer *Thanksgiving*, with her crew and her captain, and her captain's daughter Kate and her great friend Keane, leaned over under the press of wind in her sail. Her figurehead carved into a green wave, one of the million green waves on the salt road to their home in Baltimore, on the shores of America.